Pets, Paws, and Poisons

Nola Robertson

ISBN-13: 978-1-953213-14-3

Also by Nola Robertson

The Tarron Hunter Series

Hunter Claimed
Hunter Enslaved
Hunter Unchained
Hunter Forbidden
Hunter Scorned
Hunter Avenged

City Light Shifters (Stand Alone)

Stolen Surrender

A Cumberpatch Cove Mystery

Death and Doubloons
Sabers, Sails, and Murder
Cauldrons and Corpses
Pets, Paws, and Poisons

St. Claire Witches

Hexed by Fire
Spelled With Charms

CHAPTER ONE

The streets and sidewalks running along the storefront of Mysterious Baubles, my family's shop, glistened with a thin layer of white. The light snow that had started sometime during the night was continuing to fall, the cascading layers of flakes mesmerizing the longer I stared at them. The change in weather hadn't hindered the flow of traffic or the number of people strolling by.

Cumberpatch Cove wasn't like other towns along the coast of Maine. Because of the place's underlying connection to the paranormal, something I'd been skeptical about until recently, our community attracted tourists year-round. Unless a blizzard rolled through the area and shut down all travel, I knew the businesses wouldn't be impacted by the winter weather.

I opened the register and slid the cash tray into place. The instant the drawer snapped shut, a dark streak whizzed past my head and landed with a loud thump on the counter next to me. My squeak echoed through the room, and I glared at Barley, my gray and black-striped Kurilian Bobtail.

He'd been acting a little wilder than usual. Most days, he thought he was a dog, but today he'd reverted back to his feline nature. His soft fur stuck out in all directions, reminding me of a small fuzzball minus a tail—a unique trait for his breed.

This was the second time in the last half hour that he'd made his way to the top shelf on the wall behind the display case, then catapulted onto the counter. As far as I could tell, there was no obvious way to reach that height, and I still hadn't observed how he'd gotten up there.

"What's up with Barley?" Abigail Spencer asked as she unlocked the front door and flipped the sign announcing that we were open. She was my grandmother on my father's side of the family, and most people, including my friends and me, called her Grams. She had a slim figure, straight dark hair peppered with silver and cinnamon eyes that were more alert than a twenty-year-olds and never missed a thing.

"It's probably the change in the weather," Jade, one of my best friends and also an employee, said. She entered the room through the doorway leading to the rear of the building carrying a box filled with pirate paraphernalia. "My mom's schnauzer gets the same wild glint in his eyes every time there's a drop in temperature." She set the box on the counter next to me, then adjusted the cuffs on the sleeves of her silky teal shirt.

I was sure that Barley was experiencing more than a wild glint, but since this was our first winter together, I had nothing to compare his behavior with. I'd never had any pets growing up and had inherited the cat from Jessica Jenkins, or rather her ghost, near the beginning of summer. My ability to see and converse with spirits started not long after my father, the biggest supernatural enthusiast I knew, sent me a spirit seeker for my birthday.

Unaware that the gift possessed magical powers, I'd made the mistake of opening it, then ended up zapped into unconsciousness. When I woke up I had my new abilities. Now, whenever I touched an object belonging to someone who'd recently died an unnatural death—mainly associated with murder—I attracted their spirit.

Unfortunately, telling a ghost to go away wasn't an option. They couldn't move on to the afterlife until they had a resolution for their death, which meant I needed to help them or be stuck being haunted for the rest of my life. On the upside, ghostly visits weren't an everyday occurrence. I didn't get mobbed by spirits when I went anywhere in town, and I didn't have to avoid cemeteries, not that I frequented our local resting place on purpose. And the three ghosts I'd encountered and helped so far had successful outcomes.

After Barley's latest stint at flying, he stayed to get his usual scratch behind the ears, then jumped off the counter and raced down the aisles, presumably in search of things he could play with or knock off the bottom shelves. To date, my mother's bottles of herbs were his favorite. It was a good thing the containers were plastic and could take the abuse. It was also a good thing that the customers didn't seem to mind whatever my cat did. They thought he was the cutest thing ever and often encouraged his playful antics.

The small silver bell hanging above the front door tinkled, and a blast of chilly air preceded Shawna, my other closest friend, into the shop. "Good morning, everybody," she said, flashing an exuberant smile. "Look who I ran into outside." She stomped her boots on the large mat near the door, then stepped aside to let Cassie Donaby inside.

Unless she had a day off, Shawna stopped by the shop every morning on her way to work the lunch hour at the Cumberpatch Cove Cantina, though today she'd arrived a little earlier than normal. Her daily ritual included perusing the newspaper articles in the Swashbuckler Gazette and reading all of our horoscopes out loud. Since the paper was tucked under her coat sleeve, I expected her and Grams to have it spread out on the back display case in no time.

"Morning," Cassie's greeting carried the same amount

of enthusiasm as Shawna's. She dislodged the snow from her boots and removed her light tan gloves before heading towards us.

Cassie worked at Purrfectly Peculiar Pets, the only store in town that catered to all creatures, furry and otherwise, that people considered to be part of their families. The place wasn't overly large, but it had a decent selection of everything anyone needed to accommodate most pets, including tropical fish, birds, and rodents. If the store didn't carry something in stock that I needed, its staff would always be happy to order it for me.

Cassie came across my cat halfway down the nearest aisle. "Hey, Barley." She bent over to scratch his head, then, like a practiced pro, extracted her hand before he could wrap his paws and sharp little claws around her wrist. "Still not fast enough," she giggled, then stepped around him.

Shawna placed the newspaper on the counter, then pulled off a knit cap, exposing light brown curls streaked with a blue shade that happened to be her boyfriend Nate's favorite color. After shrugging out of her coat, she turned and asked, "Where's Jonathan and Caroline?"

"My guess is they'll be here shortly," I said. My parents had retired earlier in the year. They'd left me in charge of managing the shop, which included my grandmother, who had a penchant for getting into trouble. They didn't have a set schedule, but now that they were back from their latest trip to Las Vegas, I could count on them to show up to work every day.

"Are you off today?" I asked since Cassie was a full-time employee and usually worked the pet shop's morning shift.

"No, I'm actually here on store business." Cassie opened the large shopping bag dangling from her wrist. The bag had a trail of dog paws and the store's logo imprinted on the yellow plastic. She pulled out an inch-wide stack of pamphlets with a rubber band wrapped around the middle.

"Purrfectly is one of the sponsors for the Pets-R-Special Expo being held this weekend in Waxford Bay. I was wondering if you wouldn't mind setting these out for your customers."

"No problem," I said, taking the colorful stack and removing the band.

"Oooh, this looks like a lot of fun," Shawna said, snagging a flyer off the top.

"It definitely is." Cassie bobbed her head. "Purrfectly is setting up a booth. I'll be working most of the time and plan on spending the weekend to avoid commuting."

Jade and Grams gathered on Shawna's other side so they could read over her shoulder with me.

"I've never been to a pet expo," Jade said. "What exactly do they do?"

"Pretty much everything you can think of that has to do with pets." Cassie held up her hand. "Let's see. There's a food court." She touched the tip of her finger as she began listing items. "There's also a bunch of different vendors, each selling something specifically designed for pet care or competing in shows. Then there's a display area where people like to show off their champion dogs and cats. Some of them even have puppies and kittens for sale." She beamed with excitement. "That's my favorite place to hang out when I'm not working."

"Who is this Priscilla Pottsworth person?" Grams pointed at a professionally photographed image of a woman centered on the bottom of the page. The woman in the photo was smiling and appeared to be nearing her fifties.

"Are you serious?" Cassie asked. "You've never heard of her before?"

"No, is she supposed to be someone famous?" Grams gave a disbelieving snort. She'd lived in Cumberpatch her entire life and knew pretty much everyone.

When Jade and Shawna shook their heads, I didn't feel

bad for not knowing anything about the woman either.

"Very much so in the local animal competition circles." Cassie moved a little closer, eager to share. "Besides competing in dog shows, she also judges and hosts several expos a year."

Jade tapped the middle of the page. "Look, they even have a costume contest. Maybe you should enter Barley. I'll bet Shawna could come up with another great outfit for him."

For some reason, my friend loved finding new occasions to dress up my cat. I thought about the unicorn costume Shawna had gotten him for Halloween and cringed. Barley had been adorable and didn't seem to mind strutting around in the outfit. He'd even gotten numerous compliments from many of our customers.

Showing off Barley in the shop was a lot different than parading him around in front of many spectators. I automatically scanned the area, searching for my beloved cat. He'd moved off the shelf and was currently rolling around on the floor, his paws wrapped around one of his favorite playthings. The squeaky carrot with a face on the side was one of many toys I'd purchased from the pet store.

No matter how hard I tried, there was no getting Barley past the toy bin the shop had sitting next to the checkout counter. Every time we stopped to stock his food and purchase necessities, otherwise known as kitty litter and snacks, we ended up adding to his collection. He loved snatching whatever furry or plastic object happened to be sitting on top, then rolled around on the floor with it. Buying the item was easier than trying to extract his claws. I'd lost count of how many things I'd purchased for his amusement.

"I'm afraid Barley doesn't have any pedigree papers, and he's never been in a show before," I said, not bothering to mention his questionable behavior.

"That's okay," Cassie said, then grinned. "It's an

amateur costume contest. "None of the animals are registered. They're all pets."

"Really?" Shawna tapped her chin. I could tell she was already planning the trip and contemplating ideas for a new costume.

"They even have trophies and gift certificates for the winners." Cassie used her polished sales voice, trying to entice me.

I didn't think my cat had a chance of winning but watching him interact with the other contestants and their animals would definitely be entertaining.

"Waxford Bay is almost an hour away." I wasn't thrilled about having to drive back and forth, especially if the weather got worse and diminished the road conditions. Not that I couldn't handle driving on snow and ice. I preferred not having to deal with it after a long day of shopping and participating in events.

"Why don't you rent a room and stay for the weekend?" Grams asked. "If you drive down Thursday afternoon and come back on Sunday, you'll have almost three full days to play."

I was surprised my grandmother hadn't invited herself along. I hoped there wasn't an ulterior motive behind her helpful suggestion. I narrowed my eyes, half expecting her to tell me one of her psychic dreams was the reason she insisted my friends and I make the trip. All I got was an innocent smile, which concerned me even more.

"That's an excellent idea." Jade smiled at Grams, her blues eyes flickering with excitement. "It would be like a mini-vacation or a girl's weekend away, depending on how you look at it."

Staying an hour away from Cumberpatch wasn't exactly what I'd call a vacation, but I wasn't about to complain if it meant some time away from work and a break from my family. Not that I didn't love my family, but a few days without having to deal with their eccentricities sounded better the longer our discussion continued.

"What about the Christmas float committee? The first meeting is this weekend." It was one of the few committees, of which the town had many, that my mother continually volunteered me to work on that I enjoyed.

Grams tsked and flicked her wrist. "I can go with Caroline to the meeting and let you all know what you missed when you get back."

It wasn't that I didn't want to go to the expo, I didn't want to go by myself or have to leave one of my friends behind. I glanced at Shawna. "What about work?" I had a flexible schedule, and so did Jade since I was technically her boss. Weekends were busy at the restaurant, and I didn't know how Brant Delaney, the owner, would feel about Shawna taking off for a few days without giving much notice.

"For all the times I've helped Brant when he was short-staffed, I'm sure he won't have a problem with it," Shawna said, then reached into her coat pocket and pulled out her phone. "Give me a minute, and I'll let you know."

CHAPTER TWO

Waxford Bay wasn't a place my friends and I frequented. The last time we'd been there was to attend a sports event when we were still in high school. The weather was chilly, but the streets were dry. The storm that passed through Cumberpatch a few days ago had missed the quaint and much smaller town. Nonetheless, Jade, Shawna, and I had come prepared with heavy winter coats, gloves, and boots—Jade's more stylish than mine and Shawna's. My friend's obsession with fashion always extended to her footwear, sometimes even more than her outfits.

It turned out the expo was a highly celebrated event. After arriving in town late in the afternoon, I'd driven under a banner stretched across the main road and passed at least three signs with arrows telling us we were headed in the right direction. Fortunately, we were staying at the Tarnished Branch hotel, which happened to be across the street from the building where the activities were taking place.

When I'd called to make reservations, I'd been lucky to snag the last room they had available. It was a good thing the hotel had double beds and that my friends and I didn't mind sharing. I drove my car into the lot and parked as close to the hotel as possible. Barley had been curled up and was sleeping on Jade's lap. As soon as we stopped, he pushed to his feet, placing his front paws on the passenger side door to look out the window.

The two-story building had dark brown siding with a burnt umber trim. The landscape, now dormant for winter, appeared to be well-manicured. The shrubbery lining the exterior wall had lost most of its leaves, but the look didn't detract from the place's appeal. I'd bet anything the surrounding area looked spectacular in the spring and summer when everything was blooming.

"The hotel looks almost as nice as the Beaumont Inn," Jade said, trying to unsnap her seatbelt without dislodging Barley.

At the mention of the inn, I thought about Lavender and Serena Abbott, the sisters who owned and managed it. Actually, Serena owned it, a partnership she'd gained after marrying Colin Beaumont, whose family had owned the place for generations. Lavender had been my nemesis for years and got the job at the inn because of her sister.

I snatched Barley from Jade and clipped a leash to his collar before popping the latch for the trunk. "With any luck, we should have an Abbott free weekend." As far as I knew, the Abbotts didn't have any pets and wouldn't have a reason to be at the expo. It would be nice not to worry about running into Lavender. I could do without her sarcastic remarks because she thought I was a witch thanks to the ghostly shenanigans of Martin Cumberpatch, the not so famous pirate our town had been named after.

Because of my newly inherited powers, I'd inadvertently broken Martin's three-hundred-year-old curse and discovered a magical side to our community that I hadn't known existed. Even though I wasn't interested in repeating the experience, and was glad Martin had found his way to the afterlife, I had to admit there were times when I missed the annoying ghost.

"Sounds like a win to me." Jade got out of the car. She slipped the strap of her purse over her shoulder, then pulled a suitcase out of the trunk.

Neither of my friends cared for the sisters either. For some unknown reason, Lavender seemed to tolerate Shawna whenever she was around us.

"I'm looking forward to the weekend as well, but wouldn't it have been more fun if you had another one of your so-called visitors for us to help?" Shawna didn't do a very good job of keeping the disappointment out of her voice as she got out of the car.

Sometimes I wondered who was worse, Shawna or my dad. Though it had been almost two months since a ghost had popped into my life, I was looking forward to a relaxing weekend without any additional stress. Now that I thought about it, I couldn't remember the last vacation I'd been on that didn't involve being dragged to at least one haunted house or paranormal event by my father. "What happened to needing a break and all the shopping you planned to do once we got here?" I asked, reminding Shawna of the proclamation she'd made during our trip to Waxford.

I'd never been a believer, so my natural reaction after first acquiring my ghost-seeing skills had been to find a way to get rid of them. Besides doing some lengthy research on my own, I'd consulted Joyce and Edith, the owners of the Classic Broom. The sisters had ties to the witching community and assured me that being spirit free wasn't possible.

It had taken me a while to reach the point where I was okay with my gift. I had to admit I kind of liked helping spirits and was developing some decent sleuthing skills. It didn't mean I was ready to spend my time looking for new ghosts to help regularly. At least not yet, anyway. Though, after our last supernatural encounter, Shawna was determined to change my mind.

"Rylee's right. It's been a long time since we've had a

girl's weekend together without family and boyfriends to contend with." Jade stepped aside so Shawna could pull out her own suitcases. "Who knows when we'll get another chance to get away and play?"

"I know, but..." Shawna released a resigned and dramatic sigh, then balanced her suitcase on the edge of the trunk.

"But what?" Jade asked.

"Now that I've seen the hotel, and it's not the spooky building I'd imagined, I think Grams was wrong."

"Wrong about what?" I eyed Shawna suspiciously, the uneasy feeling I'd had about my grandmother's intentions skyrocketing to the level of all-out dread. Jade sensed my emotional turmoil and raised a brow.

"I overheard her talking to Mattie on the phone yesterday." Shawna frowned and held up a hand. "And no, I wasn't eavesdropping. She happened to make the call while I was standing at the counter reading the newspaper."

Mattie was one of my grandmother's closest friends and owned the coffee shop across the street from my family's store. I could always count on some kind of trouble when the two of them got together to conspire.

"What did she say during this call that you weren't purposely listening to?" Both of Jade's hands would have landed on her hips if she wasn't already holding her suitcase.

"Well." Shawna's enthusiasm had returned. "She told Mattie that she'd had one of her dreams the night before Cassie came into the store with the flyers for the expo."

"Okay, and..." I drew out the words, trying to ignore the feeling of foreboding creeping through my body.

"And the dream was about animals," Shawna said.

"Which is why she thought we should take this trip," I said. Grams was convinced that her dreams held some psychic meaning, but I'd never been convinced. The tension building in my chest got a little tighter. "She didn't happen to mention my great-great-uncle Howard as well, did she?"

"Wasn't he the mouse that was stealing your muffin when we were trying to help Jessica?" Jade asked, then smirked.

"Mouse?" Shawna's voice got a little higher. "No, she didn't say anything about a mouse." She had a phobia about rodents and spiders and immediately started checking the ground near her feet.

Since the odds of not having a ghostly encounter for the next three days were in my favor, I closed the trunk, then extended the handle of my suitcase. I wanted to go inside before Shawna decided to seek safety on my car's hood. "Come on," I chuckled. "Let's go see about checking into our room."

***

For a weekend getaway, Jade and Shawna had brought enough luggage to hold clothes for an entire week. Besides her rolling suitcase, Jade had a travel bag strapped over her shoulder. Shawna also had a travel bag and a regular-sized case, along with a smaller, flatter one made of faux leather that contained her laptop. Other than her need to continually search for information on the Internet, I wasn't sure when she thought she'd have time to use her computer during the next few days.

After shifting Barley until he released a disgruntled meow, and some less than graceful maneuvering on my part to hold the door open, we all made it inside.

The hotel's interior had a rustic appearance and showed the same level of care as the exterior. The floors and trim were done with hardwood. Off to the right, several cushioned chairs and a medium-sized sofa rested on a long rectangular rug. The slate-gray walls were decorated with pictures of landscapes, mostly beach and ocean views. Behind the wooden registration desk was a colorful sign stating that the hotel was pet friendly.

People were walking around. Those who'd recently checked into their rooms were headed to the elevators. Others were waiting to be helped by the clerks in one of the two lines near the registration desk. The hotel staff, a man and a woman, wore uniforms that consisted of a pair of black pants and a vest over a dark gold shirt.

"Nice job, Rylee," Jade said, moving to stand with Shawna and me behind an older couple waiting next in line.

"Yeah, this place is great," Shawna said. "I can't wait to see our room."

"Thanks," I said, setting Barley on the floor after looping the end of his leash around my wrist.

A family with two children stood in the line next to us. The boy was the oldest and looked to be about ten years old. The girl had freckles running along the bridge of her nose and across her cheeks. She had pigtails on both sides of her head, and I guessed her age to be around eight. She watched Barley rub against my leg, then impatiently tugged on her mother's coat. "Mom, how much longer? I want to go see the puppies and kitties."

"We'll go as soon as the nice man gives us our key, and we put our things in our room." The girl's mother sounded as if it wouldn't take much for her to lose her patience.

Just as I was about to offer letting the little girl pet Barley, the young woman assisting the family handed the father their key. The couple in front of us finished a few seconds later. When we moved up to the counter to be helped, a phone rang. The clerk greeted the caller by stating the hotel's name and introducing himself as Dylan. After listening to the person on the other end for a few seconds, he glanced in our direction and covered the mouthpiece. "I'll be right with you."

"No problem," Jade said, then removed the travel bag from her shoulder and set it on the floor.

"You want me to do it now?" Dylan snapped at the caller. "But that's not what we…" His cheeks flushed when he realized my friends and I had overheard him. "Yes, of course. I understand." He reached for a pen and pad. "What room?"

I couldn't see what he was jotting down from where I was standing but assumed it must be the room number and whatever other information the caller had given him. When Dylan finished talking, he used more force than necessary to place the phone back on the receiver. He groaned and tore the small sheet from the pad, then took a step closer to the other clerk. "Rachael, would you mind helping these ladies while I take care of this?" He stuffed the paper into his pants pocket.

"Not at all." Rachael forced a smile, clearly irritated with her co-worker. She moved aside when he hurried past her, then stepped up to the computer screen sitting on the lower counter in front of us. "Sorry about that. How can I help you?"

"We have a reservation under Rylee Spencer," I said.

Rachael's fingers danced across the keyboard. "One room with double beds and three people, correct?"

"Yes," I said.

Rachael studied the screen again. "I see you also have a special guest."

She stepped to the side so she could lean on the counter. "And you must be Barley." She smiled down at my cat and watched him swipe the dangling metal part of the zipper running along the side of my suitcase. When he heard his name, he stopped to look up at Rachael and meow. "We've never had a Kurilian Bobtail stay with us before. At least not in the three years I've worked here."

Not many people could guess what type of cat Barley was by looking at him and usually asked. Rachael must have noticed his breed listed in the information I'd submitted when completing the online registration.

"Were you able to fill my request for my cat's potty

accommodations?" I had a portable box and a spare container of litter in the trunk but hoped I wouldn't have to use them. Barley would be spending quite a bit of time in the hotel room, and I wanted to make sure he had everything he needed to be comfortable. I'd already packed his food and water bowl along with a small container of his favorite cat food in my suitcase.

"We were," Rachael said. "There's a box that looks like a cabinet underneath the sink in the bathroom that I'm sure he'll find quite suitable."

"That sounds great, thanks," I said.

"Then let's finish getting you a room." Rachael went back to staring at the screen and typing.

She spent the next few minutes checking us in and informing us about the hotel's amenities. We were each given a key with an orange plastic keyring stamped with the hotel's logo, instead of the swipe cards used by more modern establishments.

We used the elevator and arrived on the second floor in no time. After the bell chimed and doors opened, Dylan bumped into Barley and me in his haste to get inside. If my suitcase had been sitting on the floor behind me and not beside me, I would have tripped and toppled from the step I'd been forced to take backward. Barley wasn't happy about being jostled either and made some discontented kitty noises.

Dylan mumbled an apology that lacked sincerity, then turned to brace his back against the frame to hold the door open until we were out. He tapped the metal with his fingertips and kept glancing around as if he expected someone to come chasing after him.

Once we were in the hallway, I set Barley on the floor so he could walk instead of digging his nails into my arm.

Shawna continued to stare at the closed doors for a few more seconds, then asked, "Was it me, or do you think there was something up with that hotel guy?"

"He did seem a little stressed." I glanced at the

numbered plaque on the wall to see which way the arrow leading to our room pointed. "Maybe he had to deal with a guest emergency."

"Maybe," Shawna said, though she didn't sound convinced.

"You're in the foodservice business," Jade said. "You know how irritating some customers can be."

Shawna made a contemplative noise and nodded. "That's true. I remember this one time when..."

"Oh, look, our room's this way." I felt a little bad about cutting her off, but Shawna's stories tended to be lengthy. I'd rather hear the rest of it in our room, not standing in the corridor.

"Great." Shawna didn't seem to mind my interruption in the least. After adjusting her grip on her computer case, she happily trailed after Jade and me.

Our room was located toward the end of the hallway, not far from an intersecting corridor. The walls were painted the same gray I'd seen in the lobby, and the carpet was dark charcoal. The comforters on both beds had striped prints in similar shades and were accented with a light blue.

"I'll share with Jade," Shawna said, setting the bag with her laptop on one end of the dresser. "Why don't you and Barley take that bed over there?" She jutted her chin toward the bed closest to the window, then flipped her regular suitcase on its side and placed it on the floor near the wall.

I was flexible with arrangements as long as I had a place to sleep that didn't involve the floor. I'd already told my friends that Barley preferred curling up with me and refused to use the pet cushion I'd purchased for him if there was a bed available.

"Unless you want to trade for Jade and let me have Barley." Shawna giggled, ignoring the glare Jade gave her.

"Just for that, I plan on snoring in your ear all night," Jade said, placing her bags against the wall next to

Shawna's.

"Barley, it looks like we're over here." I set my suitcase on the floor on the opposite side of the dresser and my purse on the table sitting in front of the window. After placing Barley on the bed, I unhooked his leash. The instant he was free, he turned into a wild cat. He hopped from one bed to the other, then jumped off the edge and raced around the room.

When he went into the bathroom, I followed him. The kitty box was more impressive than the picture the hotel had posted on their website. Other than the wheels underneath and the hole in the door, the feline facility resembled a cabinet and blended well with the rest of the room.

Barley sniffed the exterior, then sat on the floor in front of the opening. Rather than go inside, he stared up at me and meowed. "Sorry, bud, did you want some privacy?" I backed out of the room, smiling when Barley disappeared into the cabinet and I heard him scratching the gravel.

There were pamphlets on the dresser, and I stopped to peruse them. Neatly laid out next to them were two different "Do Not Disturb" tags. One was the traditional style used by a lot of old hotels and inns in the area. The other was covered with bright yellow, purple, and blue paw prints. Stamped along the bottom were the words "Pet inside. Do not open."

"Check this out," I said, holding up the tag so my friends could see it.

"I wonder if the hotel uses these all the time or if they put them out because a lot of their guests are here for the expo," Jade said

"Either way, it's a great marketing tool." As soon as I returned the tag to the dresser, my phone started to ring. I retrieved it from my purse and glanced at the unfamiliar number displayed on the screen. I had no idea who might be calling but answered with a "Hello" anyway.

"Hi, Rylee, it's Cassie," the female voice on the other end of the call said. "I hope you don't mind, but I asked Grams for your number."

"No, not at all. Is there a problem?" I asked.

"I thought you guys might enjoy a tour. If you want, I can show you around, help you get registered for the show, and introduce you to the owners."

I repeated what Cassie said to Shawna and Jade, and after a few minutes of working out the details, we agreed on a time and place to meet.

CHAPTER THREE

A half hour after receiving the call from Cassie, my friends and I headed for the building housing the pet expo. The wind had picked up since we'd arrived, and I had to pull the collar of my coat tighter to stay warm as we walked across the street.

A large plastic banner announcing the event had been strung over the main double doors of a large brick building that looked as if it had contained several businesses at one time and been converted into a community center. It seemed Cumberpatch wasn't the only place with a town council that transformed old buildings into money-making facilities.

The building our council had chosen for our events was located next to the By the Bay Cemetery. The resting place for the dead had daily tours and attracted a lot of tourist business. The location was probably why our annual Halloween haunted house did so well.

As soon as we stepped inside, we found Cassie waiting for us. "Hey guys, I'm so glad you decided to come."

"Thanks for inviting us," I said.

"Where's Barley?" Cassie asked. "You're still planning on showing him, aren't you?"

"He's curled up and sleeping on a pillow." I wanted to check out the expo without having to worry about my cat and had left him behind.

"Great, let me give you a quick tour, then I'll show you where to register for the show." Cassie walked across the entrance area to another set of glass doors. "If you don't want to spend all your time at the expo, Waxford has a bunch of shops a few blocks away." Cassie waved her hand in the general direction of the middle of town. "There's also a dessert shop if you're interested, but it's not as good as Mattie's place."

I was definitely interested, and judging by the flicker in Jade's and Shawna's eyes, they were as well. My friends and I might differ in many ways, but coveting delectable treats was something we had in common. "I know at least one stop we'll be making tomorrow," I chuckled.

"Absolutely," Jade said. "Right after we check out a few of the shops."

"I agree," Shawna said. "I'm always on the lookout for a good sale."

I wasn't an avid shopper, not like Shawna and Jade, but I did enjoy checking out new stores. It never hurt to keep an eye on the competition, not that Waxford was close enough to be a concern. I was more interested in seeing if the local stores had any unique items that might be worth researching and adding to our shop's inventory.

Once inside, Cassie led us down a central walkway past numerous aisles of booths. "As you can see, there are a lot of vendors that participate. Some of them are still setting up and won't be open until tomorrow."

The room was full of activity, a sense of excitement filling the air. People were busy constructing their displays or making final adjustments. Others were pushing handcarts stacked with boxes. I scanned the crowd to see if I recognized anyone and spotted the woman whose picture was in the flyer Cassie had shown us. "Hey, isn't that Priscilla Pottsworth?"

The woman's straight sandy brown hair was parted on the left side of her head, touched her shoulders, and was a little longer than in her picture. She wore black pants with a matching jacket over a hunter green shirt.

"She's the person in charge of this whole thing, isn't she?" Jade asked.

"Yes, she likes to be here for the entire event," Cassie said. "She has a place about fifteen minutes from town and usually stays at the hotel so she doesn't have to drive. Come on, I'll introduce you to her."

"We don't want to bother her if she's busy." I knew from all the committees I'd worked on how hectic things could get during the organizing and set up process.

"She won't mind," Cassie said. "Trust me." She headed in Priscilla's direction, her strides brisk and determined.

Shawna giggled. "I guess we should go and meet her, then."

"We probably should," Jade said as we hurried to catch up with Cassie.

Priscilla had her back to us, and Cassie was calling out her name by the time we'd reached her.

Priscilla spun around, saw Cassie, and smiled. "Hello, Cassie, how are you?

"Fine, thanks," Cassie said.

"I saw Purrfectly's booth. Are you working or playing this weekend?" Priscilla asked.

"Hopefully, a little of both," Cassie grinned. "I know you're busy, but I was hoping you had a few minutes to meet some friends of mine who drove over from Cumberpatch to participate in the costume contest."

"Of course, I would love to meet them." Priscilla's smile, though genuine, seemed reserved. Her professional demeanor had to be a result of being a show judge for quite a few years.

"This is Jade, Shawna, and Rylee." Cassie pointed to each of us in turn. "Guys, this is Priscilla, the person in charge and the one that makes this event so much fun."

Her enthusiastic introduction was probably her way of trying to make a good impression on the older woman since she'd already provided my friends and me with the same information when she convinced us to attend.

"With my help, of course," a man said, then pushed his way between Cassie and Priscilla. After giving the rest of us a quick glance, he shifted sideways, seemingly uninterested in introductions.

He stood a few inches taller than Priscilla but had the same facial features. Black was also his color of choice, but he wore a silky red and gray vest over his shirt instead of a jacket. His face was clean-shaven except for a thin mustache, and he'd used more styling gel than Jade did in a week to keep his short wavy strands in place.

"Was there something you needed, Cameron?" Priscilla pursed her lips, not bothering to hide her annoyance at being interrupted.

"*Your* assistant let Poppy slip her collar again." He sneered as he spun a small bright pink band decorated with fake diamond studs around his index finger.

"My assistant has a name," Priscilla replied, her tone brusque.

"Yes, I'm aware," he scoffed. "But I'm your business partner, and I don't appreciate the way *Amelia* takes care of our prize-winning animals."

"I'm sure neither one of them has gone far." Priscilla held out her hand. "I'll take care of finding them."

"Fine," he said, slapping the collar in her palm, then spinning on his heels and departing the same way he came.

"I'm sorry about that." Priscilla gave us an apologetic smile. "It was nice meeting you all, but I'm afraid I have to cut our conversation short and find Amelia before Cameron does."

I waited until Priscilla was out of earshot, then asked Cassie, "Who was that?"

Cassie wrinkled her nose, apparently as unimpressed with the man as I was. "That was Priscilla's younger brother. I know he works for her, but I don't think he's really her business partner, though he likes to make everyone think he is."

Growing up in a small town, my friends and I had developed a natural inclination toward being curious. We watched Cameron walk across the room, acknowledging everyone that crossed his path with a curt nod.

Shawna shook her head and said, "Priscilla seems like such a nice person, and Cameron…"

"Seems kind of arrogant and superficial," Cassie finished for her.

"I was going to say demanding, maybe a little obnoxious, but that works," Shawna said.

I thought about the working relationship I had with my family. They might have eccentric tendencies and occasionally make me crazy, but I never regretted running the family shop with them.

After listening to the siblings interact and seeing Priscilla's scowl, it was clear that she might not feel the same way about her brother. Though I hadn't met Amelia yet and had nothing to base a comparison with, it was clear that Priscilla was protective of her assistant. Were there substantial reasons for Cameron's criticisms, or were they based on personal jealousies and dislike for the woman?

What I really wanted to know was why Priscilla would purposely choose to work with him? Was it done out of obligation or by choice? Cameron's unpleasant social skills couldn't possibly help generate business, but I didn't want to say it out loud.

Since the expo was an organized event, I assumed Priscilla and Cameron had another source of income. "Cassie, what kind of business does Priscilla own?"

"Oh, besides being a judge, Priscilla specializes in breeding champions," Cassie said. "Cameron, too, I guess. Not the judging, the breeding, and selling."

The collar Cameron had given Priscilla was fairly small, and since Cassie hadn't specified a breed, I asked, "Is

Poppy a dog or a cat?"

"She's the cutest little Pomeranian," Cassie oozed, then smiled. "She's also a grand champion, and her full name is Princess Poppy Prickle Feather."

My friends and I shared a questioning glance before Shawna blurted out, "Why would anyone want to give their dog such an odd name?"

Cassie giggled. "It's her registered show name. I have no idea where Priscilla came up with it. I do know that most show animals have unusual names."

"That's quite interesting," Jade said.

"It's a good thing I brought my computer then, huh?" Shawna smirked at Jade. "We can check it out online."

"Is Priscilla having a professional show along with the costume competition?" I asked. "I don't remember seeing anything about it in the pamphlet."

"No, but there will be a lot of breeders here this weekend," Cassie said. "It's a great way to get people interested in showing. Some of them also bring their prized animals in hopes of selling new litters or getting down payments for future breedings.

"It sounds like a lucrative business," Jade said.

"I suppose it could be," Cassie said. "From what I've heard, there are thousands of dollars involved for one animal. The price goes up depending on the lineage."

"Does the champion status play a role as well?" I asked.

"Uh-huh." Cassie nodded. "I've never been interested in showing, but I do like to play with the new puppies and kittens."

"Who is Cameron talking to?" Shawna asked.

Ever since his abrupt interruption, she'd been keeping a wary eye on him. I'd noticed because I'd been doing the same thing. He'd stopped to converse with a woman holding a small white dog. I couldn't help notice that his mannerisms appeared to be more pleasant than the interaction I'd witnessed moments ago. She didn't seem at all put off by his attitude, more like concerned by something he'd said.

Cassie glanced in his direction. "That's Luna Haysley. She's a professional groomer, supposedly one of the best in the area. From what I've heard, a lot of the show people use her for their animals, even Priscilla."

"Maybe you should see if there's something she can do about Barley's hair," Jade teased.

"Hey, I like my cat's hair just the way it is," I huffed. "His scruffy fur makes him unique."

"Speaking of Barley, why don't we get him entered in the show?" Cassie asked when she finally stopped giggling. She pointed at a long rectangular table lined with a blue skirt at the back of the room. "The registration area is over there. Come on."

We were halfway to the table when a female voice, loud and irritated, echoed in our direction. "What do you mean this is not the place to have that kind of discussion?" I turned to see a woman arguing with Priscilla. Her lips were pressed into a tight line, her cheeks flushed. She clenched her fists against her jean-clad thighs. Her long-sleeved blue shirt had some kind of logo printed below her right shoulder, but she was too far away for me to read it.

I had to give Priscilla credit for remaining calm and replying in a lowered voice. Whatever she said to the fuming woman had her stomping toward the nearest aisle, not caring that people had to scatter to get out of her way.

A younger woman with long black hair pulled back in a braid stood next to Priscilla. Her blue eyes widened, and she cuddled the tan Pomeranian she clutched in her arms closer to her chest. My assumption that the woman was her assistant Amelia was confirmed when Priscilla rubbed her forehead, then handed her the dog collar Cameron had given her.

"Oh no, that can't be good." Cassie had been watching the exchange along with my friends and me, only she'd done it with her mouth open.

When Priscilla gazed around the room, the spectators quickly returned to whatever they were doing.

"Do you know the person Priscilla was arguing with?" I asked.

"More importantly, do you have any idea what they were fighting about?" Jade asked.

"That was Naomi Birdsley." Cassie leaned closer and lowered her voice. "Some exhibitors get temperamental about their animals. I heard that the last show Priscilla judged Naomi wasn't happy that her toy poodle took third place."

"Is third place bad?" Shawna wrinkled her nose.

"It is if you were counting on your animal taking first place," Cassie said, then started toward the registration table again.

I didn't think third place sounded so bad, but I didn't make a habit of spending money to enter competitions either.

"That's the registration area over there." Cassie pointed with her chin. "The woman sitting behind the table is Melanie Hewer. She's in charge of organizing the competition and making sure all the exhibitors know what they're supposed to do."

Cassie placed her hand on my arm. "I should be getting back to the booth before my boss sends someone to look for me."

"Thanks for taking the time to show us around," I said. "We appreciate it."

Cassie took a few steps backward. "No problem, and if you get a chance, stop by the booth later. We're handing out free samples of puppy and kitty snacks."

I laughed. "If they're the ones that Barley really likes, then you can count on me stopping by."

When we reached the table, Melanie was chatting with another entrant. The middle-aged woman gripped a leash tightly as if she were afraid the small brown dog sniffing and prancing near her feet might escape any second.

While Shawna and Jade waited so we could be helped next, I stepped a few feet away to peruse an information display. The top of the panel had pictures of the animals that won in previous years. There was a wide variety of costumes, all unique and adorable. My favorites were the animals wearing cowboy, caveman, and ballerina outfits.

Tacked below the photos from the middle of the panel to the floor were several letter-sized sheets of paper with the words "MISSING" in bold, black text printed across the top. Each one had a picture of a different breed of show dog. The animal's name, information, and the person to contact if they were found was posted beneath each image. It broke my heart to think about what might have happened to someone else's beloved pet.

"The animals don't get graded on their behavior, do they?" The woman standing at the table asked. "Rexie gets a little wound up around other dogs...well, all animals, actually." She paused and glanced down at her dog. "He's still young, and the vet assured me that he'll grow out of it as he gets older."

What I'd overheard, even if unintentionally, made me think of Barley and his recent bout of wildness. It was calm in comparison to Rexie's. The dog hadn't stopped moving since we'd arrived.

"I think it depends on the judge," Melanie said. "But if you're worried, I can recommend an herbal supplement that works great for keeping animals calm."

"Oh, no, no. That's not necessary." The woman waved her free hand in the air as if giving her animal anything other than dog food was distasteful. Because of my mother's herbal remedies, I knew using them had positive effects, at least on people. I wasn't sure how well they'd work on animals.

Melanie handed the woman a white paper packet. "These are the instructions for the costume contest. If you have any questions, please don't hesitate to ask."

"I won't, and thank you."

I returned to my friends when the woman pressed the packet to her chest and strolled away from the table with Rexie tugging to get away from her.

"Welcome to the expo," Melanie greeted us with a cheerful smile. "What can I do for you?"

CHAPTER FOUR

Once we'd checked in with Melanie and gotten Barley's registration packet, Jade, Shawna, and I decided that we were too exhausted to explore Waxford. After picking up some pepperoni with extra cheese pizzas, along with some fruit-flavored wine coolers, we'd spent the rest of the previous evening relaxing in our room.

Friday morning came quickly, and after having breakfast in the hotel's restaurant, we decided to return to our room to check on Barley one last time before heading out for the day.

I'd already put out food and fresh water for him. Before we'd left, he'd finished eating and settled on the bed for a nap. I didn't think the hotel staff would be cleaning rooms on our floor until later, but as an extra precaution, I'd left the tag for pets hanging on the outside door handle.

"I'm glad we decided to do the breakfast buffet. Those waffles were excellent," Shawna said as she walked into the elevator ahead of Jade and me.

Though the waffles had looked yummy, I'd chosen to eat a bacon and cheese omelet. Normally, I could eat sweets all day long, but unlike my friend, I couldn't consume large portions of anything delectable without it instantly appearing on my hips. Not that I would say no to stopping at the dessert place Cassie had told us about when we went shopping later.

"I can't believe you ate three of them." Jade pressed the number two button.

"I thought about going for four, but I wanted to leave room in case we found something better later," Shawna said.

I pulled out the expo pamphlet I'd stashed in my purse, then after locating the schedule of events, I said, "It looks like the activities don't start until ten. What would you guys like to do until then?"

Shawna and Jade grinned at each other, then answered simultaneously. "Go shopping."

"Shopping it is," I laughed since I knew what their answer was going to be before I even asked the question.

I folded the pamphlet in half, tucked it in my back pocket, then waited for the elevator doors to open to the second floor. As soon as we reached our door, I noticed a trail of white spots running along the dark charcoal carpet in the hallway and disappearing around the corner of the intersecting corridor.

My purse slipped off my shoulder when I bent over to take a closer look. "These are paw prints." It seemed odd that the tracks were heading in our direction, then stopped in the middle of the floor. "They might belong to a dog." They weren't overly large, but they were larger than the prints I'd seen Barley make.

"So, where's the animal that made them?" Jade asked, then glanced along the hall in both directions.

"Don't you think it's weird that they stop right here, almost as if whatever made them has vanished?" Shawna raised a brow and gave me an inquisitive look.

Her mind was automatically wired to consider a paranormal presence. I didn't have to ask to know she thought a ghost had left the prints. "My special visitors are

31

usually of the human variety, and they don't leave tracks." I slipped my purse back on my shoulder as I straightened. I wasn't absolutely sure ghosts couldn't leave footprints, but since I hadn't seen any to date, I believed my information was accurate.

"Well, if that's the case, then I think we should find out where they came from." Shawna didn't give Jade and me a chance to argue. Staying near the wall and away from the prints, she followed the trail.

When we reached the end of the hallway, the path of backward paw prints veered to the right, then disappeared through an open door of the only room in the short corridor.

"Do you know who's staying in that room?" Shawna asked.

I frowned. "No clue." I wasn't sure why she thought I'd know. We'd been together since we'd arrived.

"I say we take a look in case somebody needs our help." Shawna would've raced into the room if Jade hadn't grabbed her sleeve to stop her.

"I think you should let Rylee go first." Jade tightened her grip when Shawna tried to pull away.

"Why me?" I glared at Jade, certain her suggestion wasn't a good one, not with the amount of dread I had zipping across every nerve ending in my body.

"Because I have a bad feeling about this, and you're the one with the special gift, remember?" Jade narrowed her blue gaze toward the doorway.

Arguing that being able to see ghosts wouldn't keep any of us out of harm's way if we ran into trouble that didn't involve spirits. I wasn't thrilled about leading the way, but I knew none of us would be satisfied until we'd checked inside the room to ensure the occupants were okay. "Fine," I groaned, then cautiously eased forward.

When I reached the room, I peeked around the door frame and spotted Amelia leaning against a wall, clutching Poppy to her chest, and shaking.

On the floor, not far from where she was standing, a round plastic container was lying on its side. The contents, a white powdery substance, had spilled onto the carpet. Paw prints circled the powder and created the trail that led from the room into the hallway.

I glimpsed white smudges on the front of Amelia's shirt and assumed the prints were made by Poppy. She must have picked the dog up in the hallway and carried her back to the room.

I wasn't sure what had spooked her and caused her pale complexion to lose all color. I didn't want to make things worse and slowly stepped through the doorway, then signaled Jade and Shawna to join me.

"Amelia," I said softly. "Are you okay?" If I was wrong about her identity, I was certain she'd correct me.

Amelia shrieked, then jerked her head in my direction. Poppy whined because she'd squeezed him even tighter. "Who are you?" she asked with a raspy voice. "And how do you know my name?"

"I'm Rylee, and this is Shawna and Jade." Amelia was already hugging the wall as if she were afraid we might hurt her, so I didn't move any closer. "We're here for the expo. Priscilla mentioned that you were her assistant when we met her yesterday."

Oh," Amelia said, slumping her shoulders. "I'm not okay, and I, I, think Priscilla's dead."

"What?" I asked, shocked because a dead body wasn't on the list of things I thought I'd find when I entered the room. "Where?"

Amelia lifted a shaking hand and pointed.

I'd been too focused on finding the source of the paw prints to notice the pair of heeled feet sticking out of the bathroom. I didn't want Amelia to think I was questioning her assessment, but part of me hoped she was mistaken. Maybe Priscilla had an accident and needed medical assistance. "I'm going to take a look, all right?"

"Okay," Amelia muttered.

"I'll be right back," I said to Jade and Shawna before walking further into the room.

Other than Priscilla's feet, which laid on the carpet, the rest of her body was sprawled across the bathroom's white ceramic tiles. Since the hotel room was obviously a suite, the bathroom was a lot larger than the one I shared with my friends.

Priscilla was dressed in jeans and a faded blue T-shirt. Her hair was secured at the nape, but some of the strands had pulled loose. Her dark eyes were wide and glazed over, a good indication that she was dead. If that hadn't been enough to convince me, then getting a glimpse of the contorted expression on her face, which was now a deep shade of bluish-purple, would have changed my mind.

"Amelia's right," I said without looking over my shoulder. "I don't think there's anything we can do to help her now."

"No kidding," Shawna said as she squeezed in next to me.

"I'm pretty sure we can rule out a heart attack because that doesn't look like a death from natural causes," Jade said, hovering right behind Shawna.

None of us were saying the 'M' word out loud, but by the concerned looks my friends were giving me, they were pondering the possibility that Priscilla had been murdered.

I urged Jade and Shawna to move away from the bathroom, then walked back over to Amelia, glad to see that she wasn't hugging the wall anymore. "Can you tell us what happened?" I spoke in a soothing voice.

"I don't know." A tear slipped down Amelia's cheek, and she hiccuped. "I came back to see if she needed help with anything for the show and found Poppy in the hallway. Priscilla was laying there like that when I got here."

Other than an occasional whimper, Poppy seemed relatively calm. She hadn't barked when we arrived, nor had she squirmed to get down. Animals were smart. Maybe she knew something had happened to her owner and was drawing comfort from Amelia.

"Came back?" Shawna scowled. "You were here before?"

"Yes, I brought her a breakfast tray from the hotel's restaurant." Amelia took a wary step backward. "You don't think I did this, do you?"

Amelia's guilt was something I hadn't considered until now. Did her presence mean she was responsible for her boss's death? Had Poppy escaped while she was committing the crime? Or, had she been on her way to see her boss and found the dog in the hallway like she'd said?

If Amelia was acting, which I highly doubted, she was doing a darned good job. The color still hadn't returned to her cheeks, and she seemed to be having trouble breathing. I was afraid she might start hyperventilating any second. "No one is *accusing* you of anything, are we?" Warning Shawna was unnecessary because Jade was already nudging her shoulder.

"No, I guess not," Shawna glared at Jade.

"We need to report this." My first instinct was to call Logan, but Waxford Bay was out of his jurisdiction. It was probably a good thing. I wasn't looking forward to telling him I'd been involved in finding another body.

"I'll call 9-1-1 since I don't have a number for the local police station." Jade had her phone out of her purse before I did and tapped the screen. After pressing the phone against her ear to listen, she said, "Yes, I'd like to report an incident." She paused. "It's a medical emergency...of sorts." She listened again. "No, I think it's too late for an ambulance." She gave the person on the other end of the call the location, then nodded. "Uh-huh."

Once Jade was finished, she stuck her phone back in her purse. "The police are on their way. They want us to..." She leaned sideways to see around me and frown. "Shawna, what are you doing?"

I turned and found Shawna crouching near the end of

the bed. "Getting this for Poppy." She snatched the dog's collar off the carpet and handed it to me. The latch was undone, which meant it had been removed, not slipped off by the dog.

Being a crime buff who'd watched more mystery shows than me, I couldn't believe Shawna was handling something from a potential crime scene. Even if it was the dog's collar and more than likely not used to end Priscilla's life. Before I could scold her, an electrical shock shot from the leather into my palm, then tingled all the way to my elbow.

The last time I'd experienced the same type of jolt, Grams and I had just found the body of Evelyn Fullbright clutching her deceased husband's urn. My grandmother had thrust the metal container at me hoping I'd be able to make Evelyn's ghost appear, which I had. "Shawna," I growled through gritted teeth.

"What?" She appeared confused as she used the end of the bed to get to her feet. I couldn't tell if handing me the collar had been an innocent act or if she'd given it to me expecting the same results my grandmother had. Either way, it was too late to throw the collar across the room and hope that nothing happened.

I still wasn't sure how the whole summoning spirits thing worked or how an inanimate object empowered me to see them. So far, I was convinced that touching something the newly deceased had recently handled was how we connected. At least that was my assumption.

I steadied my hand and set the collar on the floor in the spot where Shawna had found it. I'd have to explain how it ended up with our prints to whoever showed up to investigate the body. I worried that if there were any crucial fingerprints on the leather, Shawna and I hadn't messed them up.

"Oh, no," Jade said, finally catching on to why I was grimacing and flexing my fingers because they still tingled.

"Oh, yes," I said.

"No way, really?" Shawna grinned, then scanned the room as if she'd be able to see Priscilla when she arrived.

"What's going on? Did I miss something?" Amelia's gaze jumped from one of us to the other, stopping with me. "And why did you put Poppy's collar back on the floor?"

I shook my head and glanced around the room, glad the spirit I knew would be coming hadn't arrived yet. I didn't advertise the fact that I could talk to ghosts. I had no reason to believe that anyone other than Priscilla was going to make an appearance. I didn't want to have my first conversation with her in front of Amelia.

"No, everything's fine." My reassurance didn't stop Amelia from furrowing her brow even more. I guess it was understandable. Her boss was dead, and she'd been found holding Priscilla's dog and hovering near the body. Not to mention, Shawna had practically accused her of being responsible.

Amelia's grief seemed authentic, but I didn't know her personally, so there was always a chance she was faking for our benefit. Though in her defense, if she was guilty, why would she stick around and become a suspect? "The collar is part of the crime scene."

Amelia inhaled a deep breath. "I guess that makes sense."

I turned to Jade. "Why don't you and Shawna take Amelia back to our room, and I'll wait for the police here," I said, urging everyone out of the room and into the hallway.

Amelia seemed happy to comply with my request. Shawna was more reluctant and stopped in the doorway. "But I want to…"

Jade interrupted Shawna by grabbing the strap of her purse. "I really think you should come with us." She paused long enough to tell me to keep them posted, then used the strap to drag Shawna along the corridor.

As an afterthought, I called out to Jade. "You should

call the clerk at the front desk and let them know what happened, so they don't panic when the police show up."

CHAPTER FIVE

I didn't know how much time I had before local law enforcement arrived. I was confident Priscilla was going to make an appearance. I only hoped it would be soon. Dealing with a new ghost was difficult. Even more so if I was in the middle of being questioned about their murder.

Once Jade, Shawna, and Amelia were gone, and their voices had faded, I whispered, "Priscilla, are you here?" I had no idea if calling out to her would help, but I didn't think it would hurt.

Priscilla wasn't my first dead body, but I wasn't thrilled about staying in the same room with her while I waited. If I hadn't been afraid I'd inadvertently mess up a clue and end up being a suspect, I would have used the time I spent pacing near the doorway to investigate further.

It turned out my anxious period of waiting didn't last long. An immediate drop in temperature had me rubbing the sleeves of the sweater covering my arms and preceded a shimmering blue glow that manifested into Priscilla. She was wearing the same outfit she'd died in, and her hair was styled the way she'd worn it the day before.

"I remember you. You're one of Cassie's friends. Rylee, right?" Priscilla glanced around, confused. "What are you doing in my room? And where is Poppy?"

So far, the few new spirits I'd encountered were usually disoriented. They didn't know they were dead and didn't immediately remember what had happened to them. I didn't enjoy being the one to tell someone they'd died and that they were now a ghost. Even worse was having to inform them that someone they knew had committed the deed.

The only ghost who'd known where he was and how he'd gotten there was Martin Cumberpatch. His case had been different because I'd somehow released him from a curse when I'd touched his saber.

"Poppy is down the hall with Amelia," I said to alleviate her concerns about her pet. I skipped explaining how I'd ended up in her room in case she decided to ask a bunch of questions, and the conversation got lengthy.

Priscilla placed her hands on her hips. "What is she doing with Amelia? I wasn't finished grooming her."

"Um, I'm afraid that's no longer going to be possible," I said.

"What are you talking about? Why won't it be possible?"

"Because…" I stepped inside the room again, then motioned toward the feet sticking out of the bathroom.

"Who is that?" She raised her voice, pointing at the floor and wiggling her index finger. "What are they doing laying on the floor?"

"Priscilla, I'm afraid something bad happened…to you." I'd discovered that new ghosts had trouble remaining in one location shortly after arriving in this realm. I didn't want her to do what I called "poofing out" before I got a chance to ask her some questions, so I kept my voice low and tried to appear calm.

"Wait a minute. Is that me?" She stopped in the doorway and stared at the floor. "Am I dead?"

"I'm afraid so," I said, waiting for her to react hysterically, maybe do some sobbing or sniffling. What I hadn't expected her to do was walk into the bathroom and lean forward to scrutinize her body. "Why is my face such a hideous shade of purple?" She groaned. "That color doesn't go well with my outfit at all."

Seriously, she'd just found out she was dead, and the first thing she worried about was her appearance.

"Are those scratch marks on my neck?" She tried to move the loose strands out of the way, but her hand passed through her head. "Well, that's annoying."

I started to remind her that she was a ghost, then decided it wasn't worth receiving a lecture. Instead, I focused on the marks she'd mentioned. I hadn't done a thorough examination earlier and moved closer to see what she was talking about.

The long lines on both sides of her throat looked as if she clawed the skin. I wasn't an expert on causes of death, but since I hadn't seen any blood on or near her body, I felt confident I could rule out shooting, stabbing, or being bludgeoned. Had she been attacked from behind, possibly strangled? Had Priscilla tried to fight back? Was that how the marks had gotten there?

"Can you remember what happened?" I already ruled out death by natural causes. I wouldn't be standing here conversing with her ghost, otherwise.

"No, I have no idea." Priscilla squinted, her brows furrowing even further. "My memory is a bit hazy."

"That's normal," I said, pressing my palms to my thighs and stifling the urge to give her arm a sympathetic pat. I knew from experience that my hand would pass right through her and come away feeling like I'd stuck it in a freezer. The icy chill from standing next to her was a good reminder.

She eyed me skeptically, then asked in a curt tone. "How would you know?"

Though frustrating, I didn't have time to prove I knew what I was talking about or that I was the only one in the room qualified to help her. Nor did I have time to explain the intricacies of our hopefully short-lived relationship. Or how touching Poppy's collar had given me a painful jolt that enabled me to see her. "You're not my first ghost."

"Does that mean you're one of those... What are they called?" She snapped her fingers several times. "Oh yes, spiritual advisers, whisperers, or ghost detective."

She ignored my "No, not really" and continued talking. "And you're here to solve my murder, right?"

Part of her assumption had been correct. I needed to solve the crime, because if I didn't help her find the afterlife, and soon, I'd be stuck with her spirit for the rest of my life. "I suppose."

"Good, because Waxford is a small town and things like this don't happen very often. Evan is a good sheriff, but he's no detective, and neither are the people that work for him."

Just because Priscilla didn't live in town, as Cassie had mentioned, didn't mean she wasn't from the area or knew many of the locals. I'd have to take her word about how things worked here.

"Do you have a cell phone?" Priscilla asked.

"Yeah, why?" I patted my purse, unsure what she needed a phone for. It wasn't like she could call anyone.

"Then shouldn't you be taking some pictures or something?" Her glare said she couldn't believe I was acting so clueless. "Isn't that what paranormal whatever's do?"

I didn't think pointing out that I wasn't a paranormal anything would help the situation. And, after taking a second to consider her suggestion, I thought it wasn't a bad idea. Maybe not a legal one, but still a good one.

It was a risk I was willing to take if it meant helping Priscilla, so I reached inside my purse and pulled out my phone.

"Maybe you should start in here first." She gave her body another glance. "But before you do, please promise me you'll never show the pictures of me to anyone else."

"I promise I won't show anyone other than my friends, Shawna and Jade, who you met yesterday. They left a few minutes before you arrived and have already seen your unfortunate state." My friends had been adamant about helping with my other ghostly visitors, so I didn't want Priscilla to be upset if they offered to help with her death as well.

"Okay, but just them, no one else."

I swiped the phone's screen to pull up the photo app, then squatted down beside her. I wasn't necessarily squeamish, but it was unnerving to take pictures of her face with her bulging eyes staring at me. I didn't know how the people working crime scenes could do this daily without suffering from nightmares. I didn't want the reminders and planned to delete the pictures as soon as I was finished with them. Provided, of course, I was able to find the person responsible for doing this to Priscilla.

Rather than hover closer to her, I used the zoom feature to take several close-ups, then took one of her entire body and a couple more of the bathroom from different angles. With each new click, the pressure in my chest got tighter. Getting caught and ending up in jail had not been part of my plan. It would have been nice to have someone standing in the hallway and acting as a lookout. I almost wished I hadn't asked Jade and Shawna to go back to our room.

"I can't remember how that container of grooming powder ended up on the floor, but maybe you should take some pictures of it. Oh, and also the powder and paw prints." Priscilla flitted around the room as she searched for other things she wanted me to photograph. "Oh, and maybe that area over there, too." She waved her hand at a counter with a portable refrigerator and trash can tucked underneath.

The food tray Amelia had mentioned contained a covered plate and was sitting on the counter next to a portable coffee maker, the pot on the burner half empty. It seemed Priscilla had a preference in the type of coffee she drank. Next to the maker was a stack of Styrofoam cups and a plastic bowl containing several Cellophane packets of coffee stamped with the hotel's logo.

It was a good guess that Priscilla preferred using her own mug since the stack was untouched, and there was a shiny cobalt blue porcelain cup half-filled with dark liquid. The side facing me had an image of a Pomeranian. As I moved closer to get a better picture, I noticed a faint glow along the rim, which seemed to be radiating from inside the mug.

"Priscilla, what were you drinking?" I asked.

"It's my favorite French Vanilla blend. Since my expos bring in a lot of business, the owner keeps my room stocked with coffee packets.

"Has it ever glowed like that before?"

"Glowed like what?" She advanced across the room, her steps more of a glide than a walk. "I don't see anything." She stared at the cup, then wrinkled her nose as if I'd made it up.

I looked back at the cup, and the glow I'd seen was gone. "Huh, that's strange." I was tempted to swish the remaining coffee to satisfy my curiosity but tamped down the urge to avoid leaving my fingerprints behind.

Though I didn't think I'd imagined the glow, I wondered if my anxiety about being caught had affected my eyesight. In case what I'd seen had been real, I took several pictures so I could do some research later. Jade and Shawna hadn't mentioned anything, but I planned to follow up with them to see if they'd noticed something when they were in the room.

I figured half the pictures Priscilla had asked me to take had nothing to do with her demise, but I wasn't about to argue, not when I could hear voices echoing from the hallway. They were getting louder, and it wouldn't be long before I had visitors. I stopped taking pictures, keeping my focus on the doorway as I spoke to Priscilla in a lowered voice. "In case I didn't mention it, I'm the only one that can see and hear you. Something only my friends are aware of. I won't be able to talk to you, not without making others suspicious. If you have any questions, would you mind waiting until we're alone to ask them?"

Priscilla had been standing somewhere behind me, and when she didn't answer, I glanced over my shoulder and discovered that she'd disappeared. "Well, heck." Not only would I have to reiterate what I thought I'd told her, but she wouldn't be around to comment on any conversation I had with the police.

CHAPTER SIX

My assumption that the voices I'd heard belonged to local law enforcement had been correct. I received a text from Jade saying the front desk had called to let her know the police had arrived. I hadn't wanted to give them a reason to consider me a suspect, so after Priscilla vanished, I hurried out of the room and headed to the area where the two corridors met so I could see who was coming down the hallway. As it was, I'd probably receive a lecture for tampering with evidence, even though I was still convinced the collar Shawna and I handled had nothing to do with Priscilla's death.

The local official had stopped to examine the paw prints running along the carpet in the hallway. After pulling out his cell phone to take some pictures, he didn't waste any time reaching me.

He had on the same light tan uniform Roy Dixon, the sheriff of Cumberpatch wore. I guessed his age to be in the late fifties. He had a snub nose with prominent cheekbones and wore his dark silvered hair cropped short in a military style.

"I'm Evan Bresko, sheriff of Waxford Bay," the man said, his tone brusque and business-like. "My office received a call that someone found a body."

"Yes." I pointed toward the doorway at the end of the short corridor. "Down there, but..." The sheriff nodded and sidestepped around me before I could tell him that Jade, Shawna, and I walked in after Amelia found Priscilla.

Evan spent less than five minutes inside Priscilla's room before reappearing. He pointed at the officer hurrying down the hall after getting off the elevator. "This is officer Macfarland, and—"

The officer cut off the sheriff and held out his hand for me to shake. "My name's Wesley, but everyone calls me Wes." He grinned, dimples forming on his rounded cheeks.

"*Wesley,*" the sheriff groaned and rubbed his forehead.

"Sorry, sir," Wes said. Though he seemed unconcerned by the reprimand, I had a feeling the young officer got scolded a lot. "Can I take a look at the crime scene?"

"You have two minutes," Evan said.

"Great," Wes hurried past us.

"And don't touch anything," Evan ordered, then returned his attention back to me. "Are you the one that found Priscilla?" I detected a hint of sadness when he said her name.

Priscilla had mentioned that she knew the sheriff but hadn't said how well. "No, her assistant Amelia found her. She was pretty upset. I asked her to wait down the hall in the room with my friends."

"Officer Macfarland will need to take your statement while I secure the crime scene." Evan shot a sidelong glance at Wes when he returned. "Make sure you talk to her friends and Amelia as well."

"Will do, sir," Wes replied.

As soon as the sheriff disappeared back into Priscilla's room, Wes turned to me. "I have some questions. Oh, wait." He patted his shirt pocket and retrieved a small black notepad and pen. After flipping it open, he leveled a serious gaze at me. "Okay, go ahead."

I gave him a quizzical look. "You haven't asked me anything yet."

He cleared his throat. "I know pretty much everyone in town, so I take it you're not from around here. Are you visiting?"

"Yes, from Cumberpatch Cove."

He jotted something down on the pad, then asked, "Are you staying at the hotel?"

I didn't point out that I'd already said as much to the sheriff when I told him about Amelia finding Priscilla. "Yes, with my friends." I tipped my head toward Shawna and Jade. They'd come out of our room and were standing farther down the hallway with Amelia. "We're here for the pet expo." He seemed to be struggling, and since I had prior experience with being interrogated, I decided things would go a lot faster if I answered the questions I thought he might ask.

"Do you have a name?" He blushed, then quickly amended his question. "Of course, you have a name. I mean, what is it?"

"Rylee Spencer," I said, wondering how long he'd been on the job and if this was the first time he'd had to question anyone.

The sheriff must have been monitoring our conversation, or rather, eavesdropping. He peeked his head out of the room. "Did you say Spencer?"

I gave him a reluctant nod hoping he didn't have a problem with any of my relatives.

"Are you any relation to the Abigail Spencer whose family owns the Mysterious Baubles?"

My concern continued to rise and caused a knotted reaction in my stomach. "She's my grandmother. Why?" I hoped I wasn't about to pay for one of her past transgressions.

"I'll be darned." He scratched his chin and grinned.

The fact that he wasn't frowning was a good thing, so I assumed it would be okay to ask some questions. "How do you know her?"

"I met Abigail when we were both in high school. Of course, back then, the Waxford and Cumberpatch schools were rivals, but it didn't keep a bunch of us from becoming friends and hanging out together. If I remember correctly, we'd even had an adventure or two." He smiled as if he was reliving some of the memories.

"Really?" I was intrigued to learn more about my grandmother's past since she never shared the information with anyone in my family.

Evan swept his hand through the hair along the side of his head. "Did she ever tell you about the time we…"

"Excuse me, sheriff, but shouldn't I finish getting their statements?" Wes's interruption gained him another frown.

I understood wanting to make a good impression with your boss, but I was so close to getting some interesting tidbits about Grams that I found it hard not to growl at the officer myself.

"You're right." Evan straightened his shoulders, his attitude reverting back to being professional again. "When you're done with Rylee and her friends, I want you to question everyone else staying in the hotel to verify their whereabouts for the morning."

"But won't that take all day?" Wes asked, even though he didn't sound too upset by the request.

"Do you have somewhere else you need to be?" Evan asked.

"No, sir. I'll get right on it." Wes saluted with his pen.

I waited for the sheriff to go back into Priscilla's room before speaking to Wes. "Do you need to ask me your questions privately, or can you talk to my friends and me at the same time?" I wanted to hurry the interrogation along in case Priscilla decided to reappear.

"I don't suppose it matters," Wes said, motioning me to head down the hallway.

Just as we reached Jade, Shawna, and Amelia, the elevator dinged, and a man and woman stepped into the corridor with a gurney. Their jackets opened enough to expose the EMT uniforms they were wearing underneath their coats.

Waxford was probably too small to have its own medical examiner and had to use an ambulance to transport Priscilla's body. Cumberpatch, though not as large as a city, was the closest town with its own staff and capable of dealing with the dead sufficiently.

The sheriff had returned to the junction in the hallway and motioned them toward Priscilla's room. After mumbled greetings, he waited for them to pass before trailing after them. It was a good thing he'd taken pictures of the paw prints because there was no way to move the gurney down the hall without the wheels rolling over some of them.

I didn't think the tracks would remain on the carpet long after the police left anyway. The hotel management would probably have the cleaning crew remove them to keep guests from getting upset or asking too many questions.

"Officer McFarland, these are my friends Jade and Shawna," I said, tipping my head toward each of them in turn.

"You can call me Wes." He said, then held up his pad, prepared to take more notes. "Amelia, before we get started, I want you to know how sorry I am about Priscilla."

"Thanks, Wes," she rasped, then sniffled.

I wasn't surprised to hear the friendly exchange between Amelia and Wes. People that lived in a small community had a tendency to become familiar with each other.

"When I first got the call from dispatch, and they said there was an emergency at the hotel, I thought another pet had been reported missing since a lot of people brought their animals to participate in the expo. I was surprised to hear that someone had been…you know." He clicked his teeth and made a slicing motion along the front of his throat.

Hearing about stolen pets had the muscles in my chest tightening. "Have you had a lot of thefts, and should I be worried about my cat?"

"So far, only a couple of local show dogs have disappeared, so I don't think you have anything to worry about." Wes scratched his head. He was most likely afraid he'd have more than one upset female to deal with if he continued talking about the current subject. "I should finish taking statements." He looked at me as he spoke. "Why don't you start from the beginning and tell me what happened."

The elevator bell rang again, drawing the attention of the group. Cameron rushed into the hallway, pressing a hand to his chest as if he'd been winded from running.

"Wes, where's the sheriff?" Cameron asked as he hurried toward us. "Is Priscilla all right? I was across the street doing a last-minute check on the set up when I got a call from the clerk at the front desk. He said something happened to my sister."

"The sheriff's in your sister's room." Wes lowered his notepad, his smile fading. "I'm sorry to tell you this, but Priscilla's not with us anymore."

"Are you saying she's dead?" Cameron brushed past my friends and me, moving in the direction of his sister's room.

"I'm afraid so, but I can't let you go back there." Wes stepped in front of Cameron to stop him. "It's a crime scene."

"It's okay, McFarland," Evans said as he came around the corner leading the two men with the gurney that now carried Priscilla's sheet-covered body.

We all grew silent and stepped aside to make room for them to pass. I kept an eye on Amelia, afraid she might start gasping again. She stared and made cooing noises in Poppy's ear. Cameron's gaze remained locked on the gurney as it passed by us. If he was distraught about his sister's death, he wasn't showing any visible signs.

Once the EMTs reached the elevator, Evan held out his arm and spoke to Cameron. "Why don't you come with me, and I'll answer your questions?"

"Sure." Cameron sneered at Wes, then joined Evan at the end of the hall.

Instead of taking Cameron into Priscilla's room, Evan motioned him toward the left side of the adjoining corridor where our group could still see them.

I thought Wes would return to asking my friends and me more questions, but he craned his head, trying to overhear the conversation between Evan and Cameron. I couldn't blame him since I wanted to hear what they were saying as well. Jade, Shawna, and Amelia seemed equally interested and were also staring.

I could hear the two men's voices but couldn't distinguish what they were talking about, not until Cameron's outburst. "You're not going to let this shut down the expo, are you?"

"Wow," Shawna said. "Cameron doesn't seem very upset about his sister's death."

"No, he doesn't," Jade said, giving Cameron a disapproving glare.

"I wonder why." I glanced at Amelia, hoping she'd provide an answer. Working for Priscilla meant she was around the siblings all the time. If anyone knew what kind of relationship they had, it would be her.

I had to admire Amelia for her loyalty. Any personal opinions she had about Cameron she kept to herself. Wesley didn't have a problem with sharing. "I think somewhere deep down Cameron cares, but he resented her for not letting him help run the business."

"How deep do you think his emotions are buried exactly?" Shawna asked. "Because I'm envisioning a dark, murky bottomless well."

"Shawna," I scolded. My friend had a habit of voicing

her thoughts without considering their impact first.

"What...ow." Shawna rubbed her arm where Jade pinched her.

I was glad to see Amelia clamping a hand over her mouth to conceal a giggle, not bursting into tears. It was too bad Cameron had to ruin her reprieve from grieving by bellowing her name as he stomped away from Evan and returned to our group. "Priscilla's death is a tragedy, but we can't let what happened affect the expo. There are too many people counting on us. And she would have wanted us to go on."

Cameron draped his arm across the back of Amelia's shoulders. "I know it's difficult, but I'm sure you won't mind dealing with the vendors, and I'll take over all her judging responsibilities."

Amelia shrugged off his arm and stepped away from him as if his touch made her nauseous. "That's nice of you to offer, but I already called Madeline to cover."

"What, why would you do that when I could have handled the event?" Cameron stammered.

"You're still in training and not a real judge, yet," Amelia said. "And because Priscilla told me if something ever happened to her, and she wasn't able to perform, that I needed to contact Madeline immediately." She shifted Poppy in her arms so she could straighten her stance. "I called her while I was waiting for Evan and Wes to show up."

"Of course you did." Cameron ground his teeth so hard his jaw muscles twitched.

I didn't think dying had been on Priscilla's list of things that would keep her from judging. The more I listened to Cameron, the more I wanted to put him at the top of my suspect list. I could understand him not wanting to let down all the people who'd come to see the expo, but how could he not care that she was dead? I'd be mortified if something happened to anyone in my family, including my two best friends.

It was obvious that Cameron resented the attention Priscilla received, but was it a good enough reason to get rid of her? Later, if I could get Amelia alone, I planned to ask her what else she knew about Cameron's animosity toward his sister.

Amelia took another hesitant step away from Cameron. "Wes, do you suppose I could leave now? I need to take Poppy outside, or she's going to have an accident here in the hallway. You can always come to my room if you have any more questions."

Wes glanced at the squirming dog. "I guess that would be okay, but make sure that neither of you leaves town." He wiggled the end of his pen between Amelia and Poppy, then shook it at Cameron. "That includes you too, *Mr. Pottsworth.*"

It sounded like Wes wasn't impressed with Cameron either.

Cameron dismissed Wes's request with an indignant grunt, but Amelia was back to gasping again. "Are you telling me that because you think I'm a suspect? Do you think I had something to do with Priscilla's death?"

"No, it's something the sheriff asked me to relay to everyone." Wes tried to sound empathetic. "And, you are the one that found the body so…"

"Fine, okay." Amelia spun on her heels and stomped away from us.

"Wait, Amelia. I'll go with you," Cameron called after her.

"That's not necessary." Amelia didn't bother hiding a loud groan.

Once Cameron and Amelia had disappeared inside the elevator, and the doors had closed, Shawna turned to Wes. "So, officer Macfarland, any idea what happened to Priscilla?"

"Please, call me Wes." After glancing down the hallway toward Priscilla's room, he lowered his voice. "Did you notice the color of her face?"

Shawna gave him a conspiratorial wink. "It did look pretty purple. Are you thinking poison?"

"I am." Wes stuck out his chest. "There was an episode on *Suspense Beyond the Incredible* where the victim looked exactly like that."

"Oooh, I love that show." Shawna grinned. "I remember the episode you're talking about, too."

"If you're right, how long will it take to confirm whether or not someone poisoned Priscilla?" I asked. Finding out if the cause of death was caused by a toxin, and what type was used would be a clue worth knowing.

"I'm afraid it could be a week or so," Wes said. "We're a small community and aren't equipped with any cool forensic stuff. I don't know for sure about the autopsy. We'll probably have to send all the evidence somewhere else to be tested."

The news put a damper on my short-lived elation. The longer a ghost was in this realm, the harder it became to get them to the afterlife. Waiting weeks wasn't an option. I'd need to find another way to get the answers I needed to help Priscilla.

"Macfarland," Evan barked. Since his discussion with Cameron, he'd been on the phone and slipped it back into his pocket. "Don't you have some *other* guests you need to be questioning?"

"Yes, sir, I sure do," Wes said. "I'm supposed to tell you not to leave town, but since you live in Cumberpatch, it should be okay." He smiled at Shawna, Jade, and me. "Maybe I'll run into you all again later, and we can compare notes."

Compare notes? Roy and his staff had a strict policy about not sharing information with anyone who didn't wear a badge. Maybe the rules in Waxford were different. Even if they weren't, I wouldn't complain if we ran into Wes again, not if he provided us with clues that would help solve Priscilla's murder.

"Priscilla was a good friend, and I really want to catch

whoever did this to her." Wes flipped to a fresh page in his notepad, then jotted something down. He tore off the sheet and handed it to Shawna. "I don't normally do this, but if any of you think of something else that might help, please call me on my cell, okay?"

"Sure." Shawna glanced at the number, then slipped the piece of paper into her pocket.

Once Wes was out of earshot, Jade nudged Shawna's shoulder. "Wait until Nate hears how you were flirting with local law enforcement."

"I was not flirting," Shawna huffed. "I was extracting valuable information."

Shawna had a good aim if she decided to swing her purse, so I took a few steps backward before joining in the teasing. "Yeah, by flirting and getting him to give you his phone number."

CHAPTER SEVEN

Shortly after Wes left to finish interviewing other guests, Shawna, Jade, and I returned to our room. The door had barely clicked shut when Shawna asked excitedly, "So, did Priscilla's ghost show up yet? Is she here in the room with us?"

"Yes, she did, and no, she's not here," I said. "She poofed out when the police arrived, and I haven't seen her since." I dropped my purse on the dresser, then collapsed into the chair near the window. "This is not exactly what I envisioned when we decided to get away for a weekend."

Barley had been sleeping on a pillow. He lifted his head and meowed, then came over and jumped up into my lap. After kneading my thighs with his sharp claws, he made himself comfortable. I stroked his fur and contemplated everything that had happened. Having some fun and getting in some much-needed relaxation was no longer possible. Helping Priscilla was now my newest priority. "I know you guys were looking forward to going shopping, and I'll understand if you want to go without me."

"Are you kidding?" Jade set her purse on the dresser next to mine, then scratched Barley's head before settling on the bed across from me. "There's no way we'd go without you or let you try to find a killer by yourself. Besides, we can go shopping anytime."

"Jade's right," Shawna said. "What kind of friends would we be if we didn't stick around and help you?" She walked over and grabbed her small leather bag. "Besides, trying to solve a murder is way more fun." She plopped on the other bed, setting the case in front of her, then pulled out her laptop. "I knew this would be useful if I brought it along."

Jade shifted sideways so she could see Shawna as well as me. "You only brought it because you'd go into withdrawals if you couldn't play on the Internet."

"Hey, I'll have you know it's not playing. It's doing research that sometimes ends up being entertaining." Shawna looked up from the screen, a mischievous grin on her face. "Which reminds me. Now that you're officially a murder magnet, have you given any more thought to becoming a spirit sleuther?"

"I'm not." I thought about arguing that death, not me, was the magnet. I hadn't always been a paranormal enthusiast and was still adapting to things I didn't believe were real. Fate, prophecies, and anything to do with psychic revelations about the future also fell into that category. More than once since I'd received my unique abilities, I'd pondered whether or not they guided me toward locations where a death was imminent.

I didn't know how to feel about the revelation. Most of the time I ignored it, but if it really was going to continue happening, maybe my friends were right, and I needed to think about alternatives for the future.

"Actually, you kind of are," Jade said. "How many bodies did you come across before your incident with the spirit seeker?"

The answer was none, but I wasn't going to give either of them the satisfaction of being right.

"And, if you think about it, so are we. At least by association," Shawna said, returning her attention to the screen and doing some more typing.

I harrumphed like Grams. "Is a spirit sleuther even a real thing?" I'd heard the term ghost whisperer and ghost hunter used on more than one occasion, usually in conjunction with television shows that depicted both roles. I didn't think it was a real profession.

"As a matter of fact…" Shawna's fingers skimmed across the keyboard again. She grabbed her laptop and slid off her bed, then took a seat next to Jade and across from me. "Look here."

I stared at the screen, studying the website Shawna had found. Jade huddled closer so she could read along with me.

"Check this out." Jade pointed at a place near the bottom of the screen. "They even offer certification classes to get a license to become a professional sleuther."

I'd honestly never heard of such a thing, but up until a few months ago I'd never heard of a spirit seeker either. None of us had.

After everything I'd seen and learned over the past few months, I didn't think I was the only person on the planet capable of seeing ghosts. For all I knew, the certification could be a scam. It would take more than a fancy website to convince me that it was a legitimate organization.

My thoughts drifted to Logan and how he and his uncle Roy had started teasing me about finding bodies wherever I went. At one point, he'd referred to me as a spirit sleuther, but at the time I'd thought he'd made it up and was joking. It was something I planned to ask him when I got around to telling him about Priscilla's death. I could only imagine what that conversation would be like and was glad I could honestly say I didn't find the body this time.

I couldn't, however, tell Logan this incident was ghost-free. Besides my family, close friends, and a few other people with supernatural connections, he was the only other person in town that knew I could see spirits.

I really liked Logan and thought it only fair he knew about my ability before our relationship turned serious. After what happened with my last boyfriend, whose name my friends knew better than to mention, I understood the importance of trust. During Logan's last case, which happened to be finding Evelyn's killer over the Halloween weekend, I'd told him about my powers.

Surprisingly, he'd taken the news well. He wasn't happy about the investigating aspect that accompanied my situation or the fact that it sometimes put my friends and me in danger. It was an ongoing topic, or more of a non-discussion until we could come up with an agreeable resolution, one that didn't have me breaking any laws and kept me out of harm's way. On the upside, he hadn't walked away and still wanted to date, so I took it as a win.

"I think you should consider looking into the sleuther thing since you can't go anywhere anymore without stumbling across a dead body and acquiring a new spirit," Shawna said.

Leave it to my friend to state the obvious and make it sound like an everyday occurrence at the same time. "If I promise to think about it, can we focus on helping Priscilla?"

I got a "Works for me" from Jade and an "As long as you keep your promise" from Shawna.

After giving the screen another glance, Shawna asked, "Didn't you say the expo opens at ten?"

"Yeah, why?"

"That gives us about an hour to put together a list of suspects and do a little research."

This wasn't the first time my friends and I had done a brainstorming session to compile a list of people we thought had possible motives for murder.

I got up and placed Barley back on the bed, then retrieved a pad and pen stamped with the hotel's logo from inside the top dresser drawer. I'd already kitty proofed the room because of my cat's habit of making off with small objects.

"The most obvious person is Cameron. It's too bad he has an alibi," I said.

"Or so he says," Jade said. "He may have made a big production about being across the street during the time of the murder, but I think we should put him on the list until we can verify that he was telling the truth."

"I agree," Shawna said. "I think he deserves a spot just for being rude and insensitive."

"Did anyone else get the impression that Amelia didn't like him much?" I asked after jotting down Cameron's name. "I mean besides the fact that he isn't a nice person." My observation skills were decent, but getting my friend's views on a situation always helped me keep things in perspective.

"Most definitely," Shawna said. "She didn't like him at all."

"I'd sure like to know what was going on there." Jade slipped off her shoes to sit cross-legged on the bed.

"Did Amelia say anything that might be important when you were waiting in here?" I hoped that once Amelia was away from Priscilla's body she'd open up and share an important detail we could use.

"No, she was pretty quiet and most likely in shock," Jade said. "The only time she really said much was during the call she made to Madelaine."

Maybe Amelia was still afraid that Shawna thought she was guilty and decided it was best not to say anything, or she really was the one behind the crime. "I hate to say it, but we can't rule Amelia out either, not until we know for sure how Priscilla died."

"She'll more than likely be at the expo all day. We could try to talk to her once we're over there," Shawna said.

"Hey, we might even run into *officer Macfarland*. He seemed to really open up to you." Jade grinned and wiggled her eyebrows at Shawna. "Maybe you can use your newly acquired kinship to see what he found out after he questions the other guests."

Shawna glared at Jade through narrowed eyes. "I'm pretty sure if you asked, he'd share what he knows with you as well."

I was too, but it was more fun to tease Shawna and watch her squirm. Though I had a feeling it wouldn't be long before she'd gotten annoyed enough to start tossing pillows.

"I don't know about that," Jade said. "It's like the two of you had your own mystery whodunit connection."

I was right about the pillows, and when the first one flew, it missed Jade by inches and landed on the floor near my feet. Barley meowed and leaped through the air. He took refuge under the bed, which turned out to be a bad thing for anyone dangling their legs over the edge. Shawna was the closest and the first to be attacked by little paws with sharp claws.

"Barley," Shawna squealed and quickly pulled all unprotected body parts onto the bed. She ignored Jade's giggling and went back to typing. "We might also want to figure out if Priscilla has any enemies."

"That's actually a good idea," I said. "Do you have anyone specific in mind?"

"Right now, I'm researching the other expos she does throughout the year," Shawna said.

"Check to see if there's any information or posts about the dog shows she judged in the area," I said.

"Oh, and here's an article where an exhibitor accused her of improprieties at a show," Shawna said. "Apparently, the exhibitor wasn't happy that her dog didn't take first place."

"That exhibitor wouldn't happen to be Naomi, would it?" I remembered the argument Priscilla had with the woman the day before.

Shawna scrolled down the screen, then lifted her head with a grin. "It sure would."

"Do you think losing would be a good enough reason to commit murder?" I asked.

"Remember what Cassie said about people making a lot of money from selling pedigreed dogs and cats, even more if they're champions," Jade said.

Shawna's fingers flew across the keyboard again. "She's right."

I wrote Naomi's name on the list. "Cassie is familiar with the pet world. I'll bet she'd be a good resource to get more information on the gossip side of things."

"I wonder if anyone has told her about Priscilla yet," Jade said.

"If Cameron was telling the truth about being at the expo when he'd gotten the news, then there's a good chance everyone over there knows about it." I glanced at my watch. "Maybe we should go check. It looks like the expo started five minutes ago."

CHAPTER EIGHT

All the booths at the expo being set up the day before when Cassie gave Jade, Shawna, and me a tour were now open for business. There were already quite a few people milling about and shopping.

Cassie was busy helping a customer when we reached Purrfectly's booth. After waving at us, she said something to the other woman working next to her, then slipped around the makeshift counter adorned with a large black cloth covered with colorful paw prints and hurried in our direction.

Her hair was pulled back in a ponytail, and she was wearing dark pants and a long-sleeved blue shirt with the shop's logo printed below the left shoulder. "Did you hear the horrible news about Priscilla?" Cassie asked the second she joined us. Her makeup did a good job of disguising puffiness from crying but didn't hide the red in her eyes. From her interaction with Priscilla the day before, I'd gathered they were more than acquaintances.

"We did, and I'm so sorry." I placed my hand on her arm. I didn't think Cassie was aware that my friends and I had found the body; otherwise, I was sure she'd have said something.

"Thanks," Cassie said. "We weren't super close or anything, but I really liked her."

"How did you hear about what happened?" Even though Cameron told Wes he'd been in the building when he'd found out about his sister, I wasn't sure I believed him. There was something about the guy that made me wary, so I wanted to be sure he was telling the truth about his alibi.

There was a good chance Cassie had arrived early to finish setting up before the place opened. If she had, then maybe she'd seen Cameron. I wanted to find out what she knew without telling her that my friends and I considered him a suspect.

"Zoey told me." Cassie tipped her head toward her co-worker.

I didn't know Zoey all that well. I'd only interacted with her a few times when I'd visited the pet shop. She was always helpful, seemed personable, and adored Barley. If she had a problem with Priscilla, I had yet to discover what it might be.

"How did Zoey find out, and where was she at the time?" Shawna's gaze was now focused on Zoey as if she was guilty of something and should be included on our list.

Jade and I would be the first to agree that Shawna let all the mystery shows she watched influence her in real life. I didn't think there was any reason to believe Zoey had something to do with Priscilla's death, but it hadn't stopped my friend from going into interrogation mode.

Cassie seemed oblivious to Shawna's intent and more interested in gaining exciting tidbits of information. "She was in the hotel lobby on her way here when the police arrived. She asked one of the clerks what was going on, and they told her about Priscilla."

I thought about Cameron and how he'd shown up not long after Wes and Evan had arrived, stating that he'd gotten a call from one of the hotel clerks. But was it the truth? "Do you know if Zoey was the one who told

Cameron about his sister?"

"No, but she did say she saw him standing near the entrance outside arguing with someone on the phone," Cassie said. "She was going to tell him about Priscilla, but he brushed her off and stormed back to the hotel."

"Does Zoey have any idea who Cameron was talking to on the phone?" When Cameron spoke to Wes, he'd told him he was inside helping out with the expo, not outside arguing with someone on the phone. If he was outside when Zoey saw him, did that mean he'd never made it inside? Did he really receive a call from one of the hotel's clerks, or was that a lie? Did Cameron know that relatives and spouses were always at the top of the suspect list during a murder investigation? Did he have something to hide and wanted to make sure he had an alibi?

"Not that she mentioned." Cassie wrinkled her nose. "Why? Is it important?"

I shrugged. "No reason, I was curious, that's all."

"How about you guys? How did you find out?" Cassie asked.

People living in small towns were notorious for spreading rumors, and usually before verifying facts. I didn't want to give Cassie too many details about how we'd found Priscilla's body or tell her that Amelia had been there first. If Amelia was innocent of the crime, I'd rather not be responsible for someone misinterpreting anything I said and then accusing her unjustly later.

"We were on our way back from having breakfast when we found out about it," I said.

Cassie nodded. "That's right. Your room is on the same floor as Priscilla's." She glanced around as if checking to make sure we wouldn't be overheard. "Did you see anything?" Do you know what happened, or how she"—Cassie swallowed hard—"died?"

"No idea." I didn't like fabricating the truth, but I wasn't about to share the poisoning theory my friends and I were contemplating. Nor was I going to supply any details about the body's appearance.

"Have you ever met Wes, I mean officer Macfarland?" Shawna asked.

"I don't think so. Why?" Cassie asked.

"The sheriff has him talking to everyone staying in the hotel, so don't be surprised if he stops by to ask you questions."

"It will be a short conversation because I don't know anything," Cassie said, fidgeting with the hem of her shirt.

"If you hear anything else about Priscilla's death, would you mind letting us know?" I asked. Cassie liked to chat and had the advantage of knowing the people working the expo, and might possibly glean a clue or two that could help.

"Not at all." Cassie glanced back at her booth. "It looks like we're getting busy, so I better get back."

"I'll bet this place gets a lot of traffic throughout the day," Jade said.

I'd been so busy trying to get information from Cassie that I hadn't noticed the arrival of more people or the increased noise level and rumble of voices.

It was a good thing Cassie left when she did because the air surrounding us suddenly grew cold. A few seconds later, a shimmering cloud appeared and gradually transformed into Priscilla. Her entire body, including her clothes: a sweater and thigh-length skirt, remained a translucent blue.

The only thing that stood out was a tag pinned to her vest. It was black and shaped in the silhouette of a dog. Her name and the word "JUDGE" right below it were printed in the middle in bold white letters. I didn't know enough about dogs to determine which breed the tag was supposed to represent.

"Hey, Priscilla," I said low enough to alert my friends to her presence without any of the nearby shoppers being able to hear me.

She acknowledged me with a snort, then released an

exasperated sigh as she smoothed the front of her skirt. "It's a good thing you're like a lighthouse beacon; otherwise, I never would have found you."

It wasn't the first time I'd been compared to a beacon. Martin had made a similar comment when he'd been flitting around in this realm.

"It would also be nice if someone handed out instruction books to the newly departed," Priscilla huffed. "I don't like not knowing what to do or how I'm supposed to get from one place to the other without any difficulty."

It was hard not to smirk since I'd remarked on the same issue more than once. "Maybe you can mention instruction manuals to someone when you reach the afterlife." Being the only one that could hear what a spirit said was a downside to my ghostly abilities. I didn't like having to repeat everything I heard and did my best to incorporate what was discussed in my half of the conversation.

I was glad Jade and Shawna had gotten good at deciphering the details. And judging by their giggles, they'd found the topic amusing.

Priscilla gave them a speculative glance. "These are the friends who know about your gift, correct? The ones who are going to help you find my killer."

"Yes." Since Priscilla had already met them once, I didn't bother introducing them again.

Anyone who walked past us and heard me talking to Priscilla would assume I was conversing with my friends. Even so, the serious questions I needed to ask Priscilla about her murder wasn't something I wanted to be overheard.

Knowing Jade and Shawna would interpret the meaning behind my words, I turned to them and asked, "What do you think about getting out of here and grabbing an early lunch, somewhere we can talk privately?"

CHAPTER NINE

Our early lunch turned out to be ordering sandwiches and sodas from a nearby restaurant and taking them back to our hotel room where we could have some privacy. I didn't think discussing Priscilla's murder was an appropriate topic for a place that served food, not when there were children around.

Now that some time had passed, I hoped Priscilla's memory about what happened had gotten better. I had more questions and was certain Shawna and Jade did as well. Even with all the expo activity, which in the past would startle my ghostly visitors into disappearing, Priscilla managed to stay with us.

It only took minutes after I'd opened the door for the aroma from the takeout bag Jade was carrying to fill the room and draw Barley's attention. He crawled out from under the bed, then pressed his body against my legs, his purr growing louder the longer he rubbed.

Priscilla inspected Barley from one end to the other. "You have a Kurilian Bobtail?" She sounded surprised and impressed at the same time.

"I inherited him from a friend," I said, shedding my purse and coat. After taking the drinks out of the cardboard tray I'd been carrying, I set them next to the wrapped sandwiches and napkins Jade had placed on the table.

"Well, he's not show quality, but he is beautiful," Priscilla said.

"Thanks, I like him." Actually, I'd gotten very attached to my cat and couldn't imagine what life would be like without him.

"Did you enter him in the costume competition?" Priscilla asked.

"Yes, Shawna got him an outfit." I hadn't seen the costume yet because Shawna wanted it to be a surprise and refused to let me see it.

Shawna and Jade grabbed their lunch and drinks, then settled on the bed closest to the window, using pillows propped against the headboard to brace their backs.

Once I settled into a chair, Barley jumped up on my lap. "Sorry, bud, this food isn't for you." I placed him back on the floor, which didn't make him happy, and ended his purring. Knowing he wasn't going to get any scraps from me, he got up on the bed and found a place between my friends where he could sit and stare at them equally.

Priscilla's eyes flickered with amusement when she moved past me to take a seat in the empty chair across from me.

"Priscilla," Shawna asked, her gaze aimed at the spot near the dresser where the ghost had been standing when I spoke to her last.

I cleared my throat and hitched my thumb toward the chair.

"Oh, thanks." Shawna shifted her attention to the new location. "Can you tell us what you remember about the incident?"

"Incident?" Priscilla asked, slapping a hand on her chest. "Does she think my murder, the ending of my life, my ghastly demise was merely an occurrence?"

I coughed, trying to swallow the bite I'd taken without

choking. At first, I thought Priscilla's dramatic outburst resulted from being offended by Shawna's question until she raised a brow and winked at me. I never would have guessed that she had a sense of humor, especially when discussing her own death.

"Rylee, are you okay?" Jade had one leg over the edge of the bed, prepared to come to my rescue if needed.

"Food went down the wrong way." I reached for my drink, and after taking a sip, I asked, "So Priscilla, can you tell us what you do remember from yesterday?"

Priscilla stared speculatively across the room, not concentrating on anything specific. After a few seconds, her gaze returned to me. "The last thing I remember before finding you and learning I'd died was removing the lid from the grooming powder."

I repeated what she said to Jade and Shawna.

"That might explain how the powder got all over the floor," Shawna said. "Maybe something caused you to drop it, then Poppy walked through it and left prints all over the place."

"That ties into the part of Amelia's story about being on her way back to the room when she found Poppy in the hallway," I said.

"That doesn't explain how Poppy got out of the room in the first place, though." Shawna waved her half-eaten sandwich through the air before taking another bite.

"Someone would've had to leave the door open for her to get out." Jade used a napkin to wipe some excess mayonnaise off her fingers.

I glanced at Priscilla. "Did anyone besides Amelia visit you yesterday morning?"

"Not that I recall," Priscilla said.

"Is it possible you were trying to reach the door when you fell into the bathroom?" I asked. "They are kind of close to each other."

"I suppose it's possible." Priscilla frowned. "I've never had a problem with my memory before, and not being able to remember is quite frustrating."

"I'm not absolutely certain, but I think memory loss is a side effect of being a ghost." My words, though soothing, didn't seem to console Priscilla much. She still had her lips clamped together tightly.

"Don't worry, we'll do our best to figure this out." I wasn't going to say I promised because I couldn't predict the future and hated to give her reassurances I might not be able to keep.

"Are we still going with the theory that Priscilla was poisoned?" Shawna asked, glancing at Jade, then me.

After we both nodded, she continued, "Then the poison had to come from something she touched or ingested."

"I think we can rule out the collar," Jade said. "You two both handled it, and you're fine."

"We can also eliminate the powder since it came in contact with Poppy," I said.

"Not necessarily. What if it contained a toxin that is animal safe and only affects humans?" Shawna asked, then stuffed the last of her sandwich in her mouth.

"Is there really such a thing?" I couldn't help sounding skeptical.

Shawna shrugged. "I don't know, but I think it's worth finding out, don't you?"

"Are there any online sites you can check for that kind of information?" I was good at using the Internet, but when it came to unusual things, topics that no one regularly searched for, Shawna was the pro in our group.

"Probably, but you know who would be a better source, don't you?" Shawna asked.

Edith and Joyce Haverston were the two names that immediately popped into my mind. Though the sisters had been helpful in the past, I was hesitant about getting them involved. I wasn't sure if my trepidation stemmed from the uncanny way they always knew things about me or the prophetic parting words Edith was inclined to give me after each of our conversations. Or maybe it was because I'd spent the majority of my life refusing to believe in the paranormal. Or perhaps it was because I knew the sisters had ties to the witching community and were most likely magically inclined themselves.

"I still think we should check in with Wes to see if he's discovered anything," Jade said and smiled. "And not because you two have a mystery-solving connection."

"He won't know anything about the poison yet," Shawna said.

"Maybe not, but he might have discovered an angle we didn't think about," Jade said.

"That reminds me," I snapped my fingers, causing Barley to return to the spot near my feet so he could focus his begging stare on me instead of my friends.

"What?" Jade asked.

I got up and crossed the room to pull the phone out of my purse. I'd been so focused on finding out what happened to Priscilla and coming up with suspects that I'd completely forgotten to show them the pictures she'd insisted I take.

"I probably shouldn't have taken these, but Priscilla thought it might be helpful to get some pictures of everything in her room." I glanced at Priscilla to make sure she was still okay with me sharing the photos. After receiving an approving nod, I pulled the pictures up on the screen.

"Oooh, did you take some of her body?" Shawna licked her fingers and scrambled to climb off the bed.

"Yes, several of them, but you can't forward or show them to anyone else." I clutched the phone to my chest instead of placing it in her outstretched, now mustard-free hand. "I promised Priscilla I would only let the two of you see them. Once we solve the case, I'm going to delete them. Agreed?" Of my two friends, I narrowed my gaze at Shawna, specifically because she'd be the one most likely to share the pictures.

"Fine," she groaned.

I waited until I received an "Okay" from Jade before handing over the phone.

Shawna swiped the screen to make the image bigger. "Her face seems to be a darker purple than I remember."

When Priscilla cringed, I said, "Shawna, remember the discussion we had about sensitivity."

She looked in Priscilla's general direction. "Sorry, this is just...fascinating. Hey, what are those marks on her throat? I didn't see those before."

Priscilla crinkled her nose and tapped her foot, concentrating. A few seconds later, her eyes widened. "Now I remember. I had an unbearable burning sensation in my throat and couldn't talk. I was clawing my neck, thinking about getting help, and must have tried to leave the room." She dropped her shoulders and sighed. "Obviously, I didn't make it."

I didn't enjoy telling Jade and Shawna what Priscilla had said. Once I was through, I grasped for something else to talk about. "Take a look at the picture of the coffee cup sitting on the counter next to the pot." I leaned forward to look at the screen upside down while Shawna skimmed through the photos. "It might have been my imagination, or there was something wrong with the lights, because I could've sworn the liquid and the rim of the cup had been glowing."

"It looks like a regular cup to me," Jade said after squinting at the screen. "I don't see anything unusual."

"Sorry, me neither," Shawna said, after enlarging the picture even more.

"It doesn't mean you didn't see the glow or that it wasn't real," Jade said, her tone supportive.

It was nice to have friends that always believed in me. "Yeah, I guess."

"Hey, I believe you." Shawna tapped her chin and grinned. "It could have been magic, which is another good reason why you should talk to Joyce and Edith."

CHAPTER TEN

It was midafternoon by the time Jade, Shawna, and I had finished lunch and questioning Priscilla before she disappeared. Her memory of what transpired had been good, but the clues we'd obtained still weren't enough to figure out who had wanted her dead and why.

We decided the best place to find most of the suspects on our list was back at the expo. As we walked past the reception desk on our way to the building across the street, I heard a male voice calling Shawna's name. We all turned at the same time and spotted Nate, Bryce, and Myra entering the hotel's lobby through the front doors.

"Nate?" Shawna sounded as surprised as I was to see them. Even so, I glared at the group, then whispered as I leaned toward her. "Did you tell your boyfriend about you know who or where he could find us?"

"No, I swear."

"Then what are they doing here?" Jade asked, not happy to see our unexpected guests any more than I was, even if Bryce was her brother.

In comparison to Nate and Bryce, Myra was the shortest one in the group. Though they all wore jeans beneath their winter coats, Myra's red hair, green eyes, and freckles made her more noticeable. Or maybe I noticed her more readily because she rarely smiled, lacked a sense of humor, and always scowled whenever she was around me. Of the three of them, she'd been the most skeptical after learning about my ghost seeing ability.

"It's not Shawna's fault we showed up." Nate swept a hand through his sandy brown hair as he sauntered up to us. "I heard about Priscilla Pottsworth's death from a friend who lives in town. We figured since you guys were staying at the same hotel…"

"There might be some paranormal activity," Bryce finished for him. "And we decided to make the trip in case you needed our help."

Jade placed her hands on her hips, her blue eyes drilling into her brother. "You do understand the meaning of a girl's weekend out, right? That means no boyfriends, no family members,"—she included Myra and Nate when she glared at Bryce—"or club members allowed."

The club Jade was referring to was the Supernatural Spoof Squashers. Bryce had organized the group to investigate all things supernatural. Their entire membership was standing in front of us. I knew my father associated with the group, but I had yet to confirm my suspicion that he was an honorary member.

The spoofers, as Jade, Shawna, and I referred to them, were already upset with us because we'd investigated Evelyn Fullbright's death over Halloween without them. Not that we had any kind of understanding or were obligated to ask for their assistance.

Bryce held up his hands. "We didn't come here to infringe on your girl's weekend. We came to help. If you tell us nothing happened, and Rylee hasn't gotten a visitor, then we'll leave the hotel right now."

Jade might not be happy about the intrusion, but her quirked brow was her way of letting me know she'd support whatever decision I made. Shawna rocked from one foot to the other, doing her best to remain impassive, but I could tell she wanted me to be okay with the others staying, specifically Nate.

Bryce had been great about researching information for me in the past. He'd even loaned me several books on the subjects of ghosts and how to deal with their entities. Guilt and the need to be truthful guided my decision, making it difficult for me to ask them to leave. "Okay, you're right about my visitor."

"I knew it," Bryce said.

Judging by his smug grin and hands pressed tightly to his thighs, I had the feeling he'd be whooping and hollering if there weren't other people in the lobby. Our group took up a large amount of space, and a few of the guests had to walk around us to leave the building.

"Just because you have good deducing skills doesn't mean we're sharing our room with you," Jade said. "If you're planning to stay the weekend, you're on your own for sleeping arrangements."

The town only had two hotels. Since my friends and I had gotten the last room available, the spoofers would have to drive back and forth to Cumberpatch, which meant they wouldn't be able to spend a lot of time with us.

"That's okay," Nate said with a grin. "My friend Wyatt has plenty of room and already said we could stay with him."

Jade punched Bryce in the arm. "What happened to you were going to leave if we asked you to?"

"Ow." Bryce rubbed the spot she'd smacked. "I said we'd leave the hotel, not Waxford. It's not my fault if you misunderstood."

If news about Priscilla's death had reached Nate, I wondered who else back in Cumberpatch had gotten the information. Before the sibling's discussion progressed into an argument, I asked, "Did any of you talk to my family before driving over here?" I wouldn't put it past Bryce to call my father and tell him. I thought about how chaotic it would be if Grams and my parents also showed up to help. I knew they wouldn't close the shop, but they'd find a way for at least one of them to be involved in solving another murder.

"Why would we?" Myra answered for all three of them.

"Just checking." I shrugged instead of explaining the complications my family's arrival would cause. It had taken Myra a long time to believe I could see ghosts. I wouldn't say we were friendly, but the less contention I had to deal with the better.

"Rylee, do you think it would be possible to ask your friend some questions about her event?" Bryce asked.

I scanned the lobby for Priscilla and didn't see her anywhere. I'd hoped she'd make a reappearance by the time we walked across the street. "Maybe later when she's around, and in a place that's not quite so public."

I gave Dylan, the clerk I'd seen working the day we arrived, a wary glance. He was standing behind the check-in counter, and I'd caught him staring in our direction several times, then quickly drop his gaze and pretend to be working on something when he noticed me watching. Either we were making him nervous or he was interested in hearing what we had to say. My guess would be the latter.

"Got it." Bryce nodded, his brandy-colored eyes flickering with excitement.

I was glad he and the others could take a hint without having to give them any details.

"Aren't you going with us to check out the expo?" Shawna asked Nate.

"Nah, we're going to go hang out with Wyatt for a little bit and we'll catch up with you later." Nate pulled Shawna into his arms, then pressed a kiss to her forehead.

Murder or not, it was still a girl's weekend, and I wasn't happy about the intrusion. Nate seemed to understand the concept, earning him a little more of my respect. Even Logan understood the rules that applied to female getaways. The last time I'd seen him he'd given me a kiss goodbye, told me to have a great time, and that he'd talk to me when I got back.

Bryce was another matter. His obsession with the paranormal took precedence over his sister's, as well as mine and Shawna's privacy. It was why Jade threatened to strangle him regularly, and the crush he'd had on Shawna for years never went anywhere. Not that his desires were obvious, at least not to Shawna.

"If something changes and you need our help, don't hesitate to call or send a text." Bryce drug his feet as he tagged along after the others. He was probably hoping one of us would change our minds and call them back before they reached the exit.

I thought the pout was a nice touch, but after years of watching him use it on Jade I'd grown immune to the tactic. His actions hadn't affected his sister either. Jade had her arms crossed and glared at him, a sure sign she was still upset about his arrival and couldn't wait for him to leave.

Bryce, Nate, and Myra had been gone long when the door opened again, letting in another chilling breeze along with Edith and Joyce Haverston. Besides the dark tan suitcase they each rolled into the lobby, Joyce clutched an animal carrier large enough to accommodate a small dog.

I didn't bother using a pet carrier for Barley. Our first visit to the vet was the only time I'd attempted to use the miniature cage, which was now collecting dust in my bedroom closet. Barley had put up such a fight that I'd ended up with claw marks all over my arms. After that, using a leash or carrying him turned out to be the simplest way to transport my cat.

"Hello girls," Joyce said, sounding as if she'd expected to see my friends and me this far away from home.

Both women had crystal blue eyes, waist-length hair, and similar facial features. Joyce had her dark brown strands braided down her back while Edith used combs adorned with raven wings to pull her blonde strands away from her face. Most of their wardrobe must have consisted of black because I'd rarely seen them dressed in any other color. I always thought it was something they did to promote their store, but it seemed I was wrong.

"Hey, Edith, Joyce," Shawna said, her grin turning into a smirk that she purposely aimed at me.

She had to be thinking about her suggestion to ask the sisters some magic-related questions regarding the glowing cup and the unusual state of Priscilla's body. Since I'd been with my friend the entire time and knew she hadn't called the sisters, I didn't think she was responsible for their arrival.

"Didn't I tell you we'd be seeing Rylee and the girls soon?" Edith flashed Joyce a knowing smile.

I wasn't fond of coincidences and wondered if talking about the sisters earlier had sent out a psychic transmission that had somehow drawn them to Waxford. I held my breath, waiting to see if Edith was going to follow up her question with a tidbit of wisdom that made no sense and would take me a considerable amount of time to decipher.

"I never doubted you for an instant." Joyce wiggled her brows, then placed the carrier on the floor next to her feet. It was hard to tell what kind of pet they had. All I could see was a lot of black fur and a pair of big amber eyes that appeared more ominous than friendly. Normally, I'd be curious and bend down to take a closer look. Knowing the sisters, the animal could be anything, and remaining where I was seemed like the smart thing to do.

Jade had been raised with pets and didn't have the same qualms about squatting to see what kind of creature was hiding in the shadowy depths. "And who do we have here?" She stretched her fingers toward the gaps between the metal bars in the door.

I was pretty sure it was a what not a who when the animal released a low, feral growl that had Jade backing away and landing on her backside.

"Sorry." Joyce held out a hand to help Jade up. "Hades doesn't like to travel and gets a little cranky after long trips."

"He'll be much better once he gets settled and has his snack," Edith said.

After hearing his growl, I didn't think he liked people much, but I wasn't going to say anything. They'd named their cat after the Greek God of the underworld, so I wasn't going to ask what kind of snack he preferred either. Visions of chopped up raw meat in a dark bowl with his name printed in blood-red letters on the side came to mind.

"Did you come to see the expo?" Jade asked.

"Yes, and to compete in the costume contest," Edith said. "We haven't missed the last five years."

Joyce clapped her hands together. "I can't wait to see all the adorable outfits."

Since I couldn't get a good look at Hades, I wondered if cute and cuddly would apply to his costume or if he'd appear as sinister as his growls.

"I think we should check-in and take Hades to our room," Joyce said. "It's never good to leave him locked up in his carrier for very long."

"That sounds like a wonderful idea," Edith said, then turned to me. "What room are you in? We can stop by later and continue our visit. I'd be most interested to hear about your newest adventure." She smiled as if she already knew about Priscilla.

My emotions were mixed about inviting them to our room, but I didn't want to be rude and gave them the number.

CHAPTER ELEVEN

It was late afternoon by the time Jade, Shawna, and I finally returned to the expo. There were a lot more people filling the aisles and checking out the various booths.

"Any sign of Priscilla yet?" Jade asked after we entered the building.

"No, but I hope she shows up soon." I gave the surrounding area another glance in case I'd missed her. Having her around to get input when I started asking questions would be helpful and hopefully lead my friends and me in the right direction to finding her killer.

Since we were here, I planned to use shopping as a cover to do some investigating. "Where do you guys want to start?"

"How about in the back where they have all the animals?" Shawna jutted her chin toward an adjoining room. There was a large banner announcing pets and show animals for sale hanging over a wide entrance.

"Works for me. I love to play with puppies and kittens." Jade sidestepped a woman who'd stopped to wipe some chocolate from a candy bar off her little girl's face, then waited for Shawna and me to reach her. "Besides, you never know what interesting tidbits we might overhear."

The thought of cuddling some miniature animals sounded fun, but collecting more clues had a better appeal. Cameron might not have been around when Priscilla met her demise, but I still wanted to know what he was hiding and why.

I mentally ran through the other names on our list. There was a good chance that at least one of them would be in the back area. If they were, then I'd need to find a way to question them without appearing nosy or making them suspicious.

We had to pass the booth for Purrfectly Peculiar Pets. There were a lot more people hovering around and standing in line to purchase items. Cassie glanced up at the same time we walked by and acknowledged me with a wide grin. If she had any new information, I was certain she would have sent me a text or called us over to her booth. Since I could get anything they had on display during my next visit to their store, I returned her wave and kept walking with my friends.

I also wanted to have a chat with Naomi about her argument with Priscilla. I already knew she owned show dogs. It was her connection to the expo, or where to find her, that presented a problem. Cassie might know, but asking her could lead to questions I didn't want to answer.

Once we entered the room designated for animals, we stopped to take a look around. Rows of tables lined with portable cages filled the area. Two large square signs were hanging from the ceiling with wire. Each one was a different color and specified that either cats or dogs could be found below them in bold black letters.

Besides the buzz created from people talking, an occasional bark filled the air. It was easy to spot the places where kittens and puppies were available to pet by the number of children pushing past the adults to hover near the tables. So far, I didn't see any sign of Cameron, Amelia, or Naomi.

"Hey, remember the clerk that was working at the hotel

registration desk the day we arrived?" Shawna asked. "The one who was acting a little strange when we got off the elevator."

"You mean Dylan?" I wasn't sure why Shawna thought it was important, but I turned anyway to see where she was looking.

"Uh-huh," Shawna said. "Isn't that him over there talking to that groomer person?"

Jade rolled her blue eyes. "You mean Luna?"

"Yeah, her. Is it my imagination, or do they look like they could be related?" It was a good thing the people in the room were too busy paying attention to the animals to notice Shawna's obvious gawking.

I took a closer look at the two, noting a similarity in their facial features. They both had high cheekbones, dark eyes, and subtle gold highlights in their medium brown hair. "Now that you mention it. They could be brother and sister."

"Let's find out, shall we?" I would have argued against Shawna's bold, straightforward method of getting information and encouraged her to use a more subtle approach. Unfortunately, she didn't give Jade and me a chance to respond. She was halfway to the table before we could chase after her.

Luna and Dylan were standing behind a long rectangular table covered with the same dark cloth bearing colorful paw prints that I'd seen on the check-in table when I'd registered Barley with Melanie. There were neat stacks of pamphlets for Poochy Primper, which I assumed was her business, along with various leaflets on pet care and showing for beginners.

Once the older couple Luna was conversing with finished making a grooming appointment for their Labrador stepped aside, Shawna, Jade, and I moved up to the table.

"Hi, are you Luna?" I asked.

"I am," Luna said. "And this is my brother, Dylan."

She gave us a professional smile meant for potential customers. "How can I help you?"

I ignored the told-you look Shawna gave Jade and me. The answer I was about to give was waylaid by Dylan. "These are the guests that found Priscilla." There was no mistaking the disdain in his voice. I had no idea why he thought discovering Priscilla's body was a bad thing or why Luna tensed after hearing the information. Was it because my friends and I were from out of town and they thought we were guilty of the crime?

"That must've been horrible for you," Luna said. "I know her brother Cameron is devastated."

"I'm sure he is." I pretended to agree with her even though I'd already witnessed his lack of concern regarding his sister's death.

Shawna disguised her disagreement with a cough. Jade gave Shawna's back an annoyed pat. "You don't happen to know if Cameron is here, do you? We'd like to give him our condolences personally."

Dylan scowled, then said, "We haven't seen him."

"Was there something I can help you with?" Luna asked again, this time her voice was strained.

"My friend Cassie works at the Purrfectly Peculiar Pets booth. She told me you were the best groomer in town, and I was hoping you wouldn't mind helping me with my cat." I'd found that a large percentage of the time, complimenting someone worked to alleviate tense situations.

The technique I'd practiced on many difficult customers visiting my family's shop had Luna relaxing and smiling. "That was nice of her."

I needed more information about Cameron and figured the best way to obtain it was by talking to people that knew him. When I'd seen Luna and Cameron together during our tour with Cassie, they'd seemed to be more than acquaintances. Luna was already on the defensive for reasons I didn't understand, so asking her outright about

Cameron wasn't going to work.

I remembered what Shawna said about the state of Barley's hair and thought it would be an excellent way to begin a conversation with Luna. "I have a Kurilian Bobtail."

"You do?" Luna's dark eyes widened.

"He's not registered or anything, but he has wild hair, and I wondered if there was something I could do to make it more manageable. Let me show you what I'm talking about." I lifted the flap on my purse and pulled out my phone. After finding a recent picture of Barley, I held it up for her to see. Dylan seemed interested as well and leaned closer to Luna to get a glimpse.

"He really is a cutie," Luna said. Her tone sounded rehearsed, and her smile lacked sincerity. "Grooming powder is the only thing I can think of that might work. I don't sell it, but you can buy some at the booth for Naomi's Pet Emporium in the other room." Her gaze shot toward the entrance and lingered.

I sensed she was being nice because she had to and was hoping my friends and I would leave. Clearly, I wasn't going to get any more information out of her no matter how many questions I asked. "I appreciate your help." I touched Jade's arm, then signaled with my head that we should go. She, in turn, gave Shawna's sleeve a tug.

"Thanks," Shawna said, grabbing a pamphlet for Luna's business off the table before we left.

"I don't know if that was helpful or not," I said.

"The place is going to be closing in another hour." Jade gave a longing look at the puppy and kitty area, then sighed. "We should check out Naomi's booth to see if she's still here."

"I think that's a wonderful idea." Priscilla appeared, startling a squeak out of me. Her outfit hadn't changed, but the Pomeranian earrings dangling from her lobes were new. They also shimmered a yellowish gold, not blue like the rest of her.

Shawna chuckled and Jade, after stifling a giggle, said, "I take it our friend is back."

"Yeah," I groaned. I'd been getting better at not jumping every time a ghost showed up and was irritated by my reaction. I was even more annoyed that my friends still found it amusing. "And she agrees with you about finding Naomi." After their altercation, Naomi was most likely at the top of Priscilla's personal list of suspects.

After leaving the animal room, we worked our way through the crowds gathered in front of various booths. We were halfway down the main walkway when Priscilla said, "There it is." She pointed at a booth situated at the end of the aisle on our right.

A rectangular sign decorated in blues, greens, and yellows hung along the back wall and reached from one corner to another. "NAOMI'S PET EMPORIUM" was printed along the center of the sign in bold black letters. Naomi had a wide variety of accessories for pets and show animals on display. What immediately caught my eye were the tubs of the same grooming powder I'd seen spilled on Priscilla's carpet. They were stacked in a pyramid style on one end of the counter.

Naomi walked around the corner, a medium-sized cardboard box in her hand. Right behind her was Wes. "Hey, guys, hold up." I stuck out my arms to stop Shawna and Jade. So far, Wes hadn't spotted us. If he was going to interview Naomi, I didn't want to interfere.

"I thought we were going to talk... Oh," Shawna said once she saw Wes.

The chatter from conversations around us made it difficult to hear what Wes was saying to Naomi, but whatever it was hadn't made her happy. She entered the booth, then slammed the box down on the counter. "All right," Naomi snapped so loud that the people standing next to us jumped. After snatching her coat off a chair in the corner and telling the young man who worked for her that she'd be back soon, she stomped toward the exit with

Wes trailing behind her.

"What do you think that was all about?" Jade asked. "Why would Wes be escorting Naomi from the building?"

"She didn't leave in handcuffs, so there's a chance he wants to question her without creating a scene." I assumed if Wes had made an arrest, and Naomi was the real killer, then Priscilla would have poofed out already. I could feel a chill behind me and glanced over my shoulder to make sure she was still there.

"I agree," Priscilla said. "Naomi has always been an attention seeker. She enjoys being in the spotlight, even if it doesn't make her look good."

"It's too bad Wes didn't stay here where we could overhear his conversation with Naomi," Shawna said.

"I might have a way we can get the information." I shifted sideways to face Jade so I could talk to Priscilla. "I know you're still getting used to your new predicament, but how comfortable are you with your abilities?"

"They seem to be more manageable." Priscilla raised a brow. "Why, what did you have in mind?"

"Do you think you can follow Wes and Naomi to do some reconnaissance for us?" I asked.

"I can try," Priscilla grinned. "I'd tell you I'll be right back, but we both know it might not be the truth."

"Do what you can, and I'll see you when I see you," I said as she faded into nothingness.

"Do you think she can do it?" Jade asked.

I'd already explained the difficulties new ghosts experienced to her and Shawna. "She said she'd try." Priscilla seemed like a person that enjoyed a good challenge. She'd already demonstrated a driven desire to find her killer, so I had no doubt she'd be successful.

With Priscilla handling Naomi, that left two people on our list of suspects that we needed to question; Cameron and Amelia. As rude as Cameron was, getting him to talk to us presented a problem. A problem I'd need to discuss with Priscilla once she returned. If anyone would know what to say to her brother to keep him from going on the defensive, it would be her.

"Do the police think Naomi is the one that hurt Priscilla?" I didn't know Amelia had joined us until I heard a positive note in her voice. She had Poppy with her. The dog pranced and pulled on her leash, seemingly excited by all the people passing by. Amelia had replaced the collar we'd left behind in Priscilla's room with a simple blue one, which hopefully the dog wouldn't be able to slip off her head.

"I don't know," I said, knowing that might change if Priscilla was successful.

"Wes was nice and everything when he questioned me, but I still think he believes I'm the one responsible for Priscilla's death," Amelia said.

Her face had regained some color, and she wasn't sniffling, which alleviated my concern that she might have a panic attack or burst into tears.

"The sheriff told him to question all the guests, so he's probably treating everyone as if they were a suspect," I said.

"Do you really think so?" Amelia asked. She bent down to pick up Poppy who was standing on her hind legs and pawing her pants.

"We do," Jade added her support.

"Absolutely," Shawna chimed in as well.

I hadn't spoken to Wes since he'd questioned us earlier, so I had no idea who he thought killed Priscilla. Every instinct I possessed continued to assure me that it couldn't be Amelia.

CHAPTER TWELVE

Even though I'd spent the night slipping in and out of a restless sleep, mostly because my thoughts were filled with solving Priscilla's murder, Saturday morning arrived sooner than I'd expected. The pet costume contest was scheduled to occur the following morning, with all the exhibitors required to check in around ten. That left us with the entire day to do more investigating. At some point, I was sure the spoofers would want to meet to discuss what we'd discovered and how they could help, but I decided to worry about them later.

I was the first to get up, shower, and dress. After that, making coffee had been my priority. Jade was the next one out of bed, so while I waited for the coffee to brew, she took her turn in the shower. By the time she was done, I'd poured us both a cup using the stack of Styrofoam sitting near the pot and set hers on the mirrored vanity outside the bathroom.

"You are awesome, thanks," Jade said, then blew on the steaming liquid.

Our room was on the second floor and away from prying eyes. After drawing the curtains to let in some sunlight, I settled into a chair by the window. "Are you planning to get up anytime soon?" I asked Shawna since she still hadn't made it out of bed.

"Maybe," she groaned, then rolled on her side and glared at the pile of clothes she'd discarded on the floor the night before. She wasn't exactly one of the neatest people I knew and had a tendency to leave her things lying around. "Hey, does anyone know where my socks went?"

"If you'd put things away, you'd know where they were." Jade set her cup on the dresser, then walked over to her suitcase to retrieve a belt and slip it through the waistband of her pants.

"I did know where they were," Shawna said. "I could've sworn I left them on the floor next to my shoes."

Barley had a habit of snatching and playing with anything smaller than him. Items made from cloth were his favorite, which explained why my slippers always found their way underneath the bed in my apartment. "You might want to check under the bed."

Shawna leaned over the side, her blue-streaked hair almost touching the floor as she lifted the comforter to peer under the bed. "Barley, you little varmint." She stretched her arm to grab whatever she'd found. "Oh my gosh, are those my underwear?"

Barley scurried out from under the other side, the sound of claws scraping the carpet. After racing around Jade's legs, he jumped on the other bed and perched on his stomach with his ears up. His fur stuck out more than usual, and he warily watched Shawna with wide and darkened eyes.

I laughed. "I told you not to leave your suitcase open."

"I know you did, but I thought you were kidding. I didn't think your cat would actually rifle through my clothes." Shawna sat on the edge of the bed clutching her socks and a clean pair of blue silk panties. I wasn't surprised by the color since she coordinated most of her wardrobe to match her hair.

"You should let Barley come and stay with us for a

couple of days," Jade giggled. "I'll bet when Shawna runs out of socks and underwear she'll do a better job of picking up after herself."

Shawna shook the hand holding the socks at Jade. "I resent you're insinuation that I'm messy."

"It wasn't an insinuation." Jade chuckled, then plopped on the end of the bed and slipped on her boots.

"Sure, it wasn't." Shawna threw one of her socks at Jade, hitting her in the back of the head. By the time Jade got up and grabbed a pillow to throw at Shawna, she'd squealed and jumped off the bed.

Priscilla picked the same moment Shawna dashed into the bathroom to appear. The pillow Jade tossed bounced off the wall and sailed right through Priscilla's chest.

Her appearance startled me, but with all the excitement going on in the room, I hadn't jumped. I'd been holding my hand pressed over the top of the cup in case a pillow flew in my direction. I was impressed I hadn't spilled any coffee. My reflexes had improved considerably when compared to how badly my first ghostly encounter had gone after Jessica appeared in the front seat of my car while I was driving.

I was used to my friends' childish antics but wasn't sure if our ghostly visitor would be as tolerant. She surprised me with a snicker. "It's been a long time since I've been to a sleepover with friends. I'd forgotten how fun they can be."

For me, they were enjoyable as long as I remained a spectator and didn't get smacked in the head with a pillow. "Good morning, Priscilla," I said for the benefit of my friends. I also pointed in her general direction to spare Jade a frosty experience if she accidentally walked through Priscilla.

Shawna had the bathroom door opened a crack, probably contemplating a way to snag the pillow off the floor and launch it at Jade. She stuck her head back into the room long enough to say, "Hey, Priscilla, I'll be with you guys in a few minutes." A few seconds later, I heard the sound of water running and figured she was taking her shower.

I was anxious to find out if Priscilla had been able to locate Wes and Naomi and what she'd overheard. Before I could ask her, someone knocked on the door.

With the fight officially over, Jade had moved on to fixing the bed. She stopped tugging on the comforter to glance at me over her shoulder. "Were we expecting someone?"

"Not that I know of." I got out of my chair, set the cup on the dresser, and walked over to the door. I had to stand on my tiptoes to peer through the peephole and get a close-up of Joyce's face.

"Rylee, it's Joyce and Edith," Joyce said. "Can we come in?"

When the sisters said they were going to stop by, I didn't think it would be this soon. I also thought they'd call first. "Sure," I said after opening the door and stepping out of the way so they could enter. They both had their hair braided and were dressed in black shirts and pants as if they'd prepared for a military recon mission.

I picked the pillow up off the floor and tossed it on the nearest bed. Instead of vanishing as I'd expected, Priscilla had drifted to the other side of the room and was standing next to the window. The sunlight made her blue form shimmer even more. Everything except the silver earrings, which today were shaped like dog bones.

Barley had been hiding under the bed ever since things started flying. He cautiously peeked out his head, then, after determining that it was safe, crawled out and walked over to Edith and Joyce. He gave their legs a curious sniff, then proceeded to rub against them.

"Hello, Barley," Edith said as she bent over to pick him up. "You can smell Hades all over us, can't you?" The scent of another animal didn't seem to bother him or stop his rumbling purr from getting louder.

Jade finished tucking the pillow under the comforter, then walked over to join us. "Morning, ladies. Would you like some coffee?"

"No, thank you, Jade. We already had some in our room," Edith said, setting Barley back on the floor.

"What did I miss?" Shawna walked out of the bathroom with a white towel wrapped around her chest. She had her head bent and was toweling her hair with another. "Did you find out anything juicy about Naomi?" She squeaked when she saw Joyce and Edith. "I didn't know we had plans to meet this morning." She sidestepped around the sisters, grabbed some clothes out of her suitcase, then hurried back into the bathroom. "I won't be long. Don't start without me," she called as she closed the door.

"Why don't you have a seat?" I motioned to the two chairs near the window, then knelt to close Shawna's suitcase and push it closer to the wall to prevent anyone from tripping.

Edith was in the lead and looked in Priscilla's direction as she spoke. "Do you have another one of your visitors?"

"Is it Priscilla?" Joyce asked, waiting for Edith to sit before taking the seat closest to the spot where Priscilla was standing.

"Yes, and yes." I rested my backside against the dresser. Jade added more coffee to her cup, then took a place next to me.

Joyce glanced to her right. "Priscilla, we were so sorry to hear about what happened to you."

"Yes, it was terrible news," Edith added. "We want you to know we're going to do everything we can to help Rylee and the girls find the person responsible."

"You know Priscilla...personally, I mean?" It hadn't occurred to me that the women had more than a professional relationship with the woman.

"Of course, we do," Joyce said. "We've been friends for years.

"Not to mention we've attended quite a few of her expos," Edith said. "Hades really enjoys competing."

I still had no idea if the animal I'd seen in their carrier was a cat or a dog. I figured I'd find out during the show tomorrow, so I didn't risk insulting the sisters by asking.

"Rylee, please tell the sisters that I'm glad they're here, and I will miss seeing Hades," Priscilla said, her voice cracking. It was the first time since her demise that she'd sounded truly distressed about her situation.

I relayed Priscilla's message to Joyce and Edith, then asked, "How do you think you can help?"

The bathroom door burst open, and Shawna rushed into the room dressed but still barefoot and clutching some dark socks in one hand. "Okay, I'm ready." She plopped on the end of the bed. "Did Priscilla already tell you what she found out about Wes and Naomi?" She leaned forward and pulled the socks on her feet.

"Not yet," I said, glancing at Priscilla.

"I don't think Naomi did it. She ranted through most of Wes's questions but said she was setting up her booth during the time of my death." Priscilla smoothed the front of her skirt. "She gave Wes the names of at least three other expo participants that could vouch for her."

I repeated what Priscilla said to the group. "Did Wes say whether or not he was going to follow up with the other participants?"

Priscilla nodded. "I guess we'll have to scratch Naomi off the list then," Jade said.

"Not necessarily," Shawna said.

Jade tapped her thighs. "Please explain because it's a little hard to prove someone did the deed if they have an alibi."

"What if whoever did this has an accomplice?" Shawna asked.

"That's something I hadn't considered, but it does sound reasonable," I said. If she was right, then Jade and I might have to start watching more of Shawna's mystery shows with her.

"It would be a lot easier to figure out if there was more than one person if we had a motive," Jade said.

"Other than being upset about her dog not becoming a champion, can you think of any other reason why Naomi would want you dead?" I asked Priscilla.

Priscilla shook her head. "No, nothing. There are a lot of people who disagree with my placements, but I can't imagine they'd want to kill me over it."

I shared Priscilla's comments with the group.

Joyce grinned and clasped her hands in her lap. "This is exciting."

"I agree most assuredly," Edith said. "Maybe the motive you're looking for has something to do with the question you wanted to ask us." She stared at me expectantly.

It was unnerving how the sisters, mainly Edith, knew things. I didn't have to ask to know she was referring to the glow I thought I'd seen in Priscilla's cup.

Shawna pressed her lips together, trying her best not to say anything. Before she blurted out what I wanted to know, I gave the sisters a brief recounting of everything I could remember from the time we'd found the paw prints to Priscilla's appearance. I included the glowing cup but didn't mention the pictures I'd taken. One, because Priscilla didn't want anyone else to see them. And two, because I still didn't think having them was legal and didn't want to get anyone into trouble. I crossed my arms. "It's only a theory, but we think Priscilla might have been poisoned."

"Yeah, you should've seen her face," Shawna interjected. "It was an unnatural shade of purple, and she had these scratch marks on her neck." She curled her fingers and mimicked clawing her throat.

I didn't think Joyce and Edith were easily shocked, but Shawna's enactment had them gasping.

"Shawna," Jade warned. "A little less drama, please."

Instead of glaring at my friend, Priscilla snickered for the second time this morning, then clasped a hand over her mouth when she caught me staring.

Edith shared a knowing look with Joyce, then tapped her chin. "If your speculations are correct about a toxin, and based on what you've told us about the mug, it sounds like some type of magic might be involved."

Shawna's eyes widened. "You mean like a hex or something?"

"We can't say for sure until we've done some further research," Joyce said.

The stomach-knotting feeling I'd been experiencing off and on since finding Pricilla's body was back. I didn't think what the sisters had in mind had anything to do with the computer and warily asked, "What kind of research?"

CHAPTER THIRTEEN

Joyce and Edith's idea of research looked a lot like breaking into a crime scene to me. I'd made the determination long before I found myself staring at the strip of yellow police tape stretched across the door to Priscilla's hotel room. It wasn't the first time I'd been in similar situations, and somehow I had a feeling it wouldn't be the last.

With Priscilla hovering off to the side, all five of us had crowded into the short corridor.

"Shouldn't someone keep an eye on the hallway in case a hotel employee shows up to clean that other room?" Jade pointed toward the opposite end of the short hallway.

I would have done it, but I needed to help Edith and Joyce once we were inside the room.

"I'll do it. I've always wanted to be a lookout," Joyce said as she walked back toward the adjoining corridor. It's not like we were robbing a bank or anything, but that didn't stop her from pressing against the wall and peeking around the corner as if someone might try to shoot her.

"Any ideas on how we're going to get inside without a key?" I was resilient in straightforward situations, but my friends and I still ranked on the novice level when it came to the more challenging aspects of investigating. It was too bad new spirits couldn't move objects; otherwise, I'd ask Priscilla to go inside and unlock the door.

Shawna dug around in her purse, then pulled out a long rectangular black case and smiled triumphantly. "We can use the new lock pick set I bought."

I'd thought it was odd that she'd made a big deal out of getting her purse before we left our room. Now I knew why. "Where did you get those?" I wasn't aware of any stores in town that sold them.

"Online." Shawna rolled her eyes as if the answer was obvious. "With all the breaking and…I mean investigating we've been doing lately, I thought they might come in handy." She handed her purse to Jade and knelt in front of the door. "I bought them for you but wanted to test them out before I gift wrapped them."

Great, not only did helping ghosts find their hereafter affect the course of my life, but it had also impacted the lives of my friends, which now included the Haverston sisters. If I wasn't careful or changed how we did things, we'd all end up in an interrogation room. Or worse, sharing a cell together.

Jade knelt next to Shawna and studied the lock. "Do you even know how to use them?"

"Yes, I've been practicing. One of us needs to be able to open doors when Rylee becomes a spirit sleuther."

"I thought we were going to discuss that later," I grumbled.

"That's wonderful news." Edith straightened to smile at me. She'd been leaning over Shawna to get a better view. "I think you'll be great at it, and there will always be spirits in need of help."

I wasn't convinced it was an area where I'd excel but agreed with there always being ghosts who needed assistance part of her statement. I didn't think discussing a topic I'd been trying to avoid was something we should be doing right before sneaking into a crime scene.

Knowing Shawna, she'd try to solicit help from Edith by telling her about the certification she'd found on the Internet. Before she got a chance, I decided to change the subject. "So, how's it going?"

"Almost there…I think." Shawna bit her lower lip and twisted two of the picks until something inside the lock clicked. "Yes," she exclaimed when she turned the handle and the door opened.

"I'm impressed," Jade said. "I didn't think you could do it."

"I told you I've been practicing." Shawna returned the picks to their case, then got to her feet. "They work great." She tried to hand them to me, but I waved her off. I didn't want to hurt her feelings, nor did I want to discuss the possibility that I'd never use her gift. "I really don't have anywhere to put them at the moment. Why don't you keep them in your purse until we get back to the room?"

I was afraid to ask where and on which doors she'd been refining her skills. Jade must've been thinking the same thing because she didn't ask either. Since Priscilla hadn't said much since we'd arrived, I wondered if returning to the place where she died was bothering her. I waited for everyone to enter ahead of me. "It's all right if you don't want to go back inside."

"I'm fine." Priscilla straightened her shoulders. "You all are risking a lot to help me, and I have no intention of remaining behind to cower."

"Okay, then." I gave Joyce one last glance before slipping inside.

"We found Amelia standing right here holding Poppy." Shawna directed everyone's gaze to a spot on the carpet, then took a few steps farther into the room.

Jade assisted with the tour by sweeping her hand toward the area leading into the bathroom. "And Priscilla was right about here."

"I see." Edith took a moment to ponder everything she'd been told so far. "Rylee, where is the cup you were telling us about?"

"It's over here," I said, stepping around everyone. The room looked the same as it did the day we found Priscilla. The spilled powder and paw prints were exactly where I remembered seeing them, but the container, the food tray, mug, and glass coffee pot were all gone. Wes had mentioned they didn't have any forensic help, but it hadn't stopped him or Evan from collecting all the evidence. "Darn, the cup's not here."

I stepped over the prints making sure not to disturb them and glanced in the trashcan underneath the counter. Even the discarded wrapper containing Priscilla's special blend of coffee had been removed. The only things they'd left behind were the coffee maker and three unopened packets of coffee. Two of them, an orange for regular coffee and a green one for decaffeinated, were printed with the hotel logo. The other, a dark blue, contained the grounds Priscilla had requested.

"Well, that's too bad." Edith had followed me and was standing on my right. "And most likely a waste of time for the police."

"Why do you say that?" Jade asked.

"Because, if what killed Priscilla was magic in nature, none of their tests will be able to detect it."

"So, we broke in here for nothing." Shawna pouted.

A gleam of light on the blue wrapper caught my eye, and I leaned closer. "Maybe not." Speckles with the same glow I'd seen in the cup left a trail that looked like glitter had been sprinkled across the packet. "Whatever was in the cup is also on this packet." I traced the trail with my finger, making sure not to touch the wrapper.

Edith squinted. "I don't see anything."

"I can't see anything either," Priscilla said. She was also scrutinizing the packet.

Frustrated, I turned to Shawna and Jade. "Seriously? None of you can see it?"

"Sorry, Rylee. There's nothing there," Jade said.

"Me neither," Shawna said after crowding in next to Jade.

I double-blinked, then stared at the packet again only to find the glow still there. "Is there something wrong with me?" I asked Edith since she was the only paranormal expert in the room. Her concerned expression didn't alleviate my anxiety or the pressure building in my chest.

"I'm sure you're fine." Edith patted my arm. "There is a good possibility that when you broke Martin's curse, you acquired a magical boost to your ability."

"Does that mean she has powers and can cast spells?" Jade draped her arm across my shoulders.

"Oooh, it would be great if she could turn people into frogs." Shawna seemed way too happy about the prospect I hoped wasn't true.

Her obsession with frog transformation wasn't new. Jade and I had been hearing about it ever since she'd had a bad break-up when we were younger. As a matter of fact, we'd accompanied her to the Classic Broom in search of a potion. Of course, at the time, I didn't believe anything paranormal really existed, so I didn't see any harm in her quest.

Priscilla's chuckle drew me from my musing. "I really like your friend. She has quite an imagination."

I refrained from repeating what Priscilla said or from telling the ghost that Shawna wasn't kidding. "Edith, please explain."

"I don't think you need to worry about spells or frogs." Though Edith attempted to hide her amusement, there was a hint of humor in her voice. "I can't be sure, but it sounds like you're able to see residual magic."

"If you're right, will this new ability fade, or will I have it forever?" I asked.

"I have no idea, but it will be fun finding out, don't you think?"

"I suppose." I wasn't nearly as resistant to the idea of seeing magical properties as I had been about being able to see spirits.

"Rylee, not to diminish the excitement about your newly found abilities, but maybe we should get going before someone catches you in here," Priscilla said.

"Priscilla thinks we should leave before we get caught," I said to the others.

"I'm in total agreement with that plan," Jade said, taking a step closer to the door.

I hated to leave empty-handed. "Edith, do you think we can still figure out what was used to poison Priscilla from the glowing spots I can see on the coffee wrapper?"

Edith rubbed her chin. "I believe it's possible."

"Great, then I think we should take the packet with us," I said.

"What if Wes and Evan come back looking for it?" Shawna asked.

"They've already collected evidence, so I doubt they'll be coming back for anything else," I said.

"Good point." Jade glanced around the room. "Now, all we need is something we can use to pick up the packet in case your little glowing spots are poisonous."

"Wait." Shawna had her purse open again and was moving things around inside. She pulled out a pair of rubber gloves and a plastic Ziploc bag, then kept the bag and handed the gloves to me.

"Do I even want to know what else is in there?" I shook my head, slipping the thin white latex over my right hand.

"Probably not," Shawna smirked. "You know how I like to be prepared. After I overheard Grams's conversation with Mattie, I wasn't sure what to expect. I brought a few things in case we ended up on another one of your missions."

"Priscilla, I'm curious." I picked the packet up by the corner farthest from the spots.

"About what?" Priscilla asked.

"Who else knew about your special blend of coffee?" I

placed the packet in the plastic bag Shawna held out to me. After pulling off the glove, so it was inside out, I dropped it in the bag as well.

"Let's see," Priscilla said. "Cameron, Amelia, and I suppose most of the hotel staff."

Repeating everything was getting tiresome, but I shared what she had to say anyway.

"That's a lot of people," Shawna said. She sealed the bag and stuffed it in her purse.

I followed the group toward the door. "And not much help in narrowing down the killer's identity. It would've been nice if only two or three people knew about the coffee." There was still a chance the poison, or whatever had killed Priscilla, had been in her food, though I had my doubts now that I'd found the presence of magic.

Cameron might have an alibi, but he also had access to his sister's room ahead of time. Amelia found the body, which could have been an act, but I didn't believe it. Trying to figure out what motive a hotel employee might have, or who it might be, bordered on the impossible and was making my head hurt.

We'd just left the room when Joyce rushed toward us hysterically swinging her arms and motioning toward the adjoining hallway. "We have to hide. I caught a glimpse of that young man who was working at the registration desk yesterday getting off the elevator."

Unfortunately, with Priscilla's room being at the end of a short corridor without any outlet, we had nowhere else to go. "Well, we can't go back to our room, not without being seen." If there was only one or two of us, pretending we got turned around might have worked to explain what we were doing near the crime scene. A group this size was too obvious, and we couldn't risk being reported to the sheriff.

"We definitely can't hang around out here either," Jade said.

Luckily, I hadn't shut the door to Priscilla's room yet,

so we didn't have to waste time using the pics on the lock again. "This way." I urged everyone back inside, then hurried to stick the strip of tape that had come loose back on the outside door frame.

After we were all inside, I kept the door open a crack listening for any signs of movement. It wasn't long before I heard voices and footsteps. Dylan wasn't the only one who'd gotten off the elevator. It sounded like Amelia was with him, and they were headed in our direction.

I closed the door as quietly as possible and slowly backed away until I bumped into whoever was standing behind me. When I turned, I found everyone hovering in a tight cluster near the entrance to the bathroom. Everyone except Priscilla. She must've been startled by all the excitement and disappeared.

I jerked my head, my pulse racing faster when I heard a key turning in the lock. "Quick, we need to hide," I whispered.

"In here." Shawna had already crossed the room and was sliding the closet door open.

It was a tight fit, but somehow we all managed to wedge into the limited space. I ended up with my chest pressed against the door. I was afraid if someone decided to check inside we'd all fall out and end up in a pile.

I didn't move or say anything. Neither did anyone else. If I had super hearing, and the pounding in my ears wasn't already loud, the noise from everyone else's racing hearts would be deafening.

"I really appreciate you letting me in here," Amelia said.

"Not a problem, but we need to hurry because if anyone catches us I could lose my job," Dylan said, his voice strained.

"I won't take long. I promise," Amelia said. "I need to get Poppy's box of toys. She's really upset and misses Priscilla."

"Are you and Poppy still planning to attend the costume competition tomorrow?" Dylan asked.

"Attending might be part of my job, but I wouldn't miss it. Besides, I think it will help Poppy to be around other animals, even if she has to stay in her carrier while I work."

I could hear footsteps getting closer and held my breath. Hopefully, the toys Amelia mentioned weren't on the shelf above our heads. Otherwise, our already awkward situation was going to get worse. The footsteps stopped, then started again a few seconds later. "Got it," Amelia said.

"Why don't you go ahead," Dylan said. "After I lock up, I've got some other guest-related items I need to take care of."

"Okay, and thanks again," Amelia said.

I heard the door close and was about to escape from the closet when I heard footsteps moving around inside the room again. I was curious to know why Dylan hadn't left and wished I could open the door slightly to see what he was doing.

"It's not here," he snarled, then followed it by saying, "Because I'm not an idiot, and I already checked." His voice got louder with each word, and it took me a minute to realize he was talking to someone on the phone. Whatever the person on the other end of the line said to him next had him slamming the door on the way out of the room.

I'd reached the point where I couldn't take being stuck in a confined area any longer. "I'd say they're gone, wouldn't you?" I spoke to the group as I opened the door, not caring if anyone agreed with me.

"Was that Amelia and Dylan we heard?" Jade asked after gulping in air as if she'd been holding her breath the whole time.

"It sounded like them to me," I said.

"Do you think he was after the coffee packet?" Shawna asked.

"Could be, but whatever he was searching for, he didn't

find it." Dylan had been talking loud enough for everyone to hear the outcome of his search. I glanced around to see if anything looked out of place or was missing. "I think we should go before someone else shows up."

No one hesitated to follow me or rush down the deserted hallway. Once we got back to our room, and everyone was safely inside, I slumped against the back of the door, my tension slowly fading.

"That was quite exhilarating," Joyce said, patting her chest. "Now I see why you girls enjoy sleuthing so much."

There were quite a few words I would have used to describe the situations my friends and I seemed to find ourselves in lately, but enjoyable wasn't one of them.

My short-lived relief didn't last long. Music from a text Shawna received on her phone rang throughout the room, causing all of us to either scream, gasp, or jump. I was thankful the message hadn't arrived while we were all crammed in the closet. I could only imagine what would have happened if Dylan had discovered us.

Not that he could report us to management without getting into trouble himself for being in Priscilla's room. It would, however, tip him off that we were investigating Priscilla's death and give him a reason to be even more wary of us than he'd been when we spoke to Luna.

Now that Shawna had stuffed the plastic bag containing the coffee packet in her purse, it took her longer to find her phone. "It's from Nate," she smiled after reading the screen. "The guys want to know when we can meet up."

"Rylee, what do you think?" Jade asked.

Our close encounter with being caught had affected all of us, even Jade. Her irritation about the prospect of spending time with her brother had diminished a lot since the day before.

I glanced at all the expectant faces, wondering why they were all staring at me or how I'd suddenly become the one in charge. "I don't have a problem getting together." I held up my hand to stop Shawna from typing a response to Nate. "But not until we've had something to eat." The spoofers were going to ask a lot of questions, and I wouldn't be able to think clearly or provide decent answers until my stomach stopped rumbling.

CHAPTER FOURTEEN

Caffeine coupled with stress wasn't a good combination. It made me jittery and left me with the beginnings of a headache. After nearly being caught by Dylan and Amelia during our visit to Priscilla's room, my friends and I, along with the Haverston sisters, agreed that anymore investigating would need to be done after we'd had breakfast.

Thanks to our excursion, we'd missed the early morning crowd in the hotel's restaurant. Most of the tables were empty, so we found one in a back corner where we didn't need to worry about our conversation being overheard by others.

After several pancakes smothered with blueberries and a cup of coffee, I was feeling a lot better and ready to discuss what we'd found and how we were going to deal with it. Or, more specifically, how Edith and Joyce were going to help us with the magical aspects I'd discovered.

"Now that we know Dylan's involved, what should we do?" Shawna pushed her empty plate aside and reached for her cup. "It's not like we can report him to the police. Not without some real evidence." She patted her purse, which was hanging on the back of her chair over her coat.

Her inference that the bag containing the coffee packet she still had stashed inside wasn't going to be enough. Especially, if Edith and Joyce were right about forensic tests not detecting a magical poison that so far only I could see.

"We don't know for sure that he is involved, only that he was searching for something in Priscilla's room." Rather than discuss our growing list of suspects, I decided it might be better to focus on the source of what had taken Priscilla's life. "If we can confirm what was used, then we might be able to uncover more about the who and the why."

Time constraint was also a concern. By early afternoon tomorrow, the expo would be over, and we'd be heading home. If my friends and I didn't solve Priscilla's murder by then, I wasn't sure what I was going to do.

"I agree with Rylee." Jade tapped her fingernails against her porcelain cup. "We can't make any assumptions until we know about the glowing stuff she found."

I looked across the table at Joyce, then at Edith who was sitting next to me. "Do either of you have any suggestions on how we can go about that?"

I knew the scowl on Joyce's face when she looked at Edith was due to the situation and not because her sister had done anything to gain her disapproval. "I wish I would've thought to bring along some of our potions."

"Why is that?" Shawna propped her elbows on the table and leaned forward, eager to hear what Joyce had to say.

"To test the residue on the wrapper, of course," Edith said.

"I would suggest testing the grounds as well," Joyce said. "If it were me, that's where I'd put the poison. A tiny hole underneath the folded seal on the wrapper would work."

Edith gave her sister a thoughtful nod. "Absolutely. No one would ever suspect they were brewing a deadly cup of coffee."

I was concerned about the direction the conversation was going, not to mention worried about the additional thought the sisters were giving to planning someone else's demise.

Debra, our waitress, picked that moment to return carrying a coffee pot. Her blonde hair was pulled back in a ponytail, and she wore a burnt orange uniform with a black apron tied around her waist. "Does anyone need a refill?" If she'd overheard Edith's comment, her cheerful smile wasn't showing any signs of it. After topping off everyone's cup, she set the pot on an adjacent table. "Can I get you anything else?"

We'd all ordered a large breakfast, and other than Shawna, who'd consumed way more than Jade and me, I'd be surprised if anyone wanted anything else. When no one said anything, I glanced around the table to make sure before answering. "No, I think we're good, thanks."

"You ladies have a nice day, then." She placed the separate checks we'd asked for when we ordered facedown on the end of the table. Once she removed our plates, stacking them like a pro on one arm, she grabbed the pot again and was gone.

"Okay, so what do we do now?" I sighed. Any exhilaration I'd felt about the coffee packet, or the wrapper the police had taken into custody, as being the source of the poison was fading. "No one is going to believe us if we can't prove what was used to off Priscilla."

"Don't worry." Edith gave my arm a gentle squeeze. "We can go shopping for the supplies we need to determine what type of toxin was used."

"We should visit the Mystical Moon," Joyce said. "I'm sure they'll have what we need."

"What is the Mystical Moon?" Shawna asked. "I've never heard of it before."

I'd never heard of the place either and hoped it wasn't another name for a coven of witches.

"It's a quaint little shop on the outskirts of Waxford," Edith said, smiling. "If you like our store, then you'll love the place."

Shawna rubbed her hands together. "I can't wait."

For me, visiting the Classic Broom was something I did out of necessity, not because I was interested in potions or the variety of paranormal items the sisters had lining their shelves to entice tourists. If the Mystical Moon had the same ominous feel to it, then I wasn't eager to make the trip. Finding the source of whatever had been used to poison Priscilla was the only way we were going to find her killer. Since the sisters were willing to help us, I wasn't about to turn them down either. I pushed my phobia aside and said, "Then we should head over there next."

With more enthusiasm than I'd expected, everyone got up and donned their coats to face the winter weather outside. It didn't take us long to pay the waitress working the cash register by the door and head for the lobby.

We'd barely taken a few steps into the room when a boisterous "Hey, everybody" echoed through the air. Bryce pushed out of a chair near the wall where he was sitting with Myra and Nate and strolled over to us.

Shawna glanced at me and Jade, a deep red rising on her cheeks. "Did I forget to mention that they were on their way here and said they'd wait for us in the lobby?"

Jade glared at Shawna. "I thought we agreed to meet with them later."

"Nooo, Rylee said after breakfast." Shawna tucked a blue-streaked strand behind her ear. "And, we're finished eating sooo…"

Bryce ignored us and smiled at Edith and Joyce. "I wondered if you were going to bring Hades for the costume contest."

"He never misses a show," Joyce said.

"And, if I recall, he's taken first place in most of them," Bryce said.

Proud grins appeared on both of the sister's faces. I

didn't know what kind of costumes the judges liked, but after seeing the black furry creature inside their carrier, I'd bet anything that Edith and Joyce dressed their cherished pet in paranormal outfits. A demon, vampire, or werewolf costume was the first thing that came to mind.

"How was breakfast?" Nate asked, changing the subject as he slipped his arm around Shawna's waist.

"Great." Shawna smiled, leaning into him. "This place makes wonderful French toast."

"And how many slices did you have?" Nate asked.

"Only three, but I could've easily gone for four."

Nate chuckled. "Of that, I have no doubt."

Myra crossed her arms and impatiently tapped her right foot. "I didn't come all the way to Waxford to listen to you two get all mushy over breakfast, so if you're finished, do you suppose we can get an update on the, uh, situation?"

To say Myra and Shawna tolerated each other would be an exaggeration. Before my friend said or did something to draw attention to our group, I stepped between them. "Why don't we discuss this outside?"

"That sounds like a plan." Bryce was quick to assist by aiming Myra toward the front entrance. I couldn't tell if he was helping in order to keep Myra and Shawna apart or if he was anxious to hear what we'd learned about Priscilla.

CHAPTER FIFTEEN

After leaving the hotel's lobby, our group spent the first fifteen minutes sitting inside Edith and Joyce's minivan in the parking lot, waiting for the vehicle to warm up. We discussed what we'd learned so far with the spoofers, a conversation that continued during our drive.

"So, let me see if I'm hearing you correctly. You can now see magical..." Bryce perched excitedly on the edge of his seat, his gaze shooting from me to Edith. "What did you call it?"

Edith was driving and glanced over her shoulder. "Residual essence."

Joyce shifted sideways in the front passenger seat. "At least that's what we're assuming."

"Is that why we're going to the Mystical Moon?" Nate asked.

"Yes. Lavinia Oleander, the shop's owner, has experience with these types of things," Edith said.

Edith and Joyce hadn't said that Lavinia might be a witch, but I thought it was a good possibility since I'd learned the Mystical Moon was an apothecary shop. One that specialized in rare and unusual herbs and potions.

"I don't suppose she has psychic abilities and can give

us the name of the person that killed Priscilla, can she?" Myra scowled from her seat in the rear. For someone who'd joined a paranormal group and claimed to believe in all things supernatural, she was one of the worst skeptics I'd ever met. There were times when she made the pre-ghost seeing version of myself look good.

"I'm afraid we don't know of anyone quite that talented," Joyce responded in a pleasant voice. If she'd noticed Myra's sarcasm, she was ignoring it.

Jade was sitting next to me and leaned closer. "Speaking of Priscilla, I haven't felt a chill since our near-miss with Dylan." She glanced at the empty spot beside Shawna, who was sitting next to Nate. It was the likeliest place for Priscilla to be if she was hitching a ride with us. "Has she reappeared yet?"

Edith concentrated on making a left-hand turn onto a side street while the rest of the group listened intently to what I had to say. "Not yet, but I'm sure she'll show up soon." Summoning a spirit on command wasn't one of my abilities, and I couldn't predict when they'd arrive.

Any further questions were put on hold when Edith said, "We're here" as she parked the vehicle in one of the ten spots available in a small corner lot.

"Are you sure this is a shop?" I asked Edith and Joyce after piling out of the van with everyone else. The place seemed warm and inviting. It also looked like a residence instead of a place of business. The main entrance, a wooden door at the center of the building, looked like something out of a medieval fairy tale.

The dead vines growing up from the flower beds in front of the building clung to the exterior walls. They looked like the type of plants that sprouted vivid green leaves and beautiful blossoms during the spring and summer. There were chalet-style windows on both sides of the front door. The words Mystical Moon, along with stars and half-moon symbols, were carved into the wooden sign hanging above the entrance.

Before either of the sisters could answer, the door opened and two young women, each carrying plastic bags with the Mystical Moon logo stamped on the side, stepped out. "This place is fantastic. I'm definitely coming back here the next time we're in town," one woman said to the other.

I heard a low rumble and couldn't figure out where it was coming from until the woman closest to us adjusted the front of her coat and a Chihuahua peeked out from inside. All I could see of the dog was its small head. It was white except for a brown spot covering the area around its right eye. "It's okay, baby," she cooed at the dog and smiled as she walked past us.

When we reached the entrance, I noticed a small sign mounted next to the door that said, "Pets welcome." It seemed the whole town was animal friendly and supported Priscilla's expo.

A bell jingled as soon as Edith pushed on the door. Once we were inside, I took a moment to gaze at the aisles lined with shelves noting that the interior had a similar layout to my family's shop. The air was filled with spices and vanilla aroma as if someone had recently burned some scented candles. The place was as appealing inside as it was outside, and everyone in the group seemed to forget we were on a mission and started exploring.

One corner at the back of the shop was dedicated to books. The shelves were lined with titles referencing all kinds of magical and paranormal entities. I wasn't surprised that Bryce had bypassed everything else in the room to explore the contents. He had quite a collection of old books stored in his basement, which was officially considered the spoofer's headquarters.

"What a cool place," Shawna said, picking up a green glass bottle from a display labeled with a potions sign. She flashed a mischievous smile at Jade. "Should I see it they have a love potion you can give Kevin?"

Kevin was Evelyn Fulbright's nephew. We'd met him

around Halloween shortly after his aunt was murdered. He'd recently relocated his art gallery to Cumberpatch and shown a reciprocated interest in Jade.

"I don't need a potion to help with my love life," Jade huffed. "Maybe you should get something for Nate."

Nate was standing in the next aisle reaching for an herbal remedy. His hand froze when he heard his name. "I don't need anything, thanks." He flashed Shawna an uneasy smile, uncertainty creeping into his voice. "Do I?"

Shawna sneered at Jade as she walked over to join Nate and slipped her hand in his. "No, you're fine."

"Whew, glad to hear it," Nate said, then placed a chaste kiss on top of her head.

Footsteps echoed from a hallway located between some display cases sitting on the opposite side of the room. A woman who appeared to be in her early thirties walked through the entryway. Light gold ringlets were pulled away from her rounded face with hair combs, their tips brushing her shoulders. Numerous silver bracelets, the metal resembling thin braids, adorned her right wrist. Her outfit consisted of a long dark blue dress, slimming on her hips and adorned with a colorful scarf tied around her waist.

"Edith, Joyce, it's so good to see you again," the woman said as she approached us.

"Lavinia," Edith said, holding out her arms. "How are you?"

"Wonderful, thanks." When Lavinia finished giving each of the sisters a hug, she greeted the rest of us with a beaming smile. "Who are your friends?"

Edith pointed, giving Lavinia each of our names. I was standing on the far right of our group and was the last person to be introduced. Lavinia studied me closely, her dark eyes flickering with interest. "You've recently acquired a gift." She raised a brow. "The ability to speak with spirits, correct?"

It wasn't the first time I'd heard the comment. I'd

gotten the same kind of reaction from Edith and Joyce when I'd visited their shop not long after my encounter with the spirit seeker. I didn't know if Lavinia was a witch or a psychic. Nor did I know if there was a proper protocol for dealing with a magically inclined person. I didn't want to be rude or chance ending up as one of Shawna's favorite reptiles, if that was possible. Instead of asking her how she knew I could see ghosts, I mumbled, "Yes."

"I can sense that you're not here to shop, so what can I help you with?" Though Lavinia sounded concerned, her smile seemed genuine and never faded.

Bryce might not have come along to buy anything, but he'd found two leather-bound books I was certain would be leaving the store with us.

"Since you're aware of Rylee's gift, then you know that she is responsible for assisting spirits to their afterlife." We were currently the only customers in the place, which was why Edith didn't try to be covert about our mission when she asked her question.

"I am," Lavinia said. "If you don't mind me asking, whose spirit are you trying to help?"

"Priscilla Pottsworth," I said. "Did you know her?"

Lavinia's smile faltered. "I don't think there's anyone in Waxford that doesn't know her." Her saddened gaze dropped to the floor. She took a deep breath, then added, "Or did anyway."

"Do you think someone got rid of Priscilla to shut down the expo?" Bryce asked.

It was a motive none of us had considered, and I was impressed that Bryce had come up with it. Besides the possibility that Dylan was involved, which I still needed to prove, and the glowing speckles, we hadn't found anything substantial that would tell us why someone wanted Priscilla gone.

Lavinia shook her head. "I don't think so. Her expos attract a lot of tourists and bring additional money to the local businesses."

"What about Cameron?" I asked. "Do you think he could have done it?" If Lavinia knew Priscilla, she had to know her brother. Even if she didn't know Cameron well, people in small towns were great about snooping and sharing what went on in everyone else's personal lives.

"I suppose it's possible. Cameron's not exactly the nicest person to deal with. Although, from what I've heard, he couldn't run a business if he tried." Lavinia absently moved an herbal container on a nearby shelf, lining the label up with the other bottles. "Amelia's the one that did all the organizing for Priscilla, so I'm not sure what he'd gain by his sister's death."

"Yes, but according to the Universal Whodunit Guide, if the circumstances are right, anyone can commit murder," Shawna said.

"That's also true," Nate said as if he'd spent the same amount of time that Shawna had searching the Internet for information.

Any other time, I would've enjoyed an in-depth discussion about people's motivations for wanting someone dead, but time was quickly dwindling. "Maybe so, but it's not the real reason we're here." I looked at Edith, hoping to gain her assistance in explaining what we needed.

Edith didn't require any further encouragement. "Joyce and I believe that Rylee has also acquired the ability to see residual essence."

"Really." Lavinia's eyes widened. "That is interesting. Tell me what you saw, and don't leave anything out."

Tedious as it was, I spent the next few minutes explaining everything from finding the body and the glowing cup to obtaining the coffee wrapper tucked inside Shawna's purse. Lavinia seemed like a nice person. I didn't know her personally and didn't want to implicate Dylan or Amelia by telling her about their visit to Priscilla's room. I also didn't feel comfortable sharing how we'd hidden from them in the closet. Thankfully, no one else in our group felt inclined to share either.

"Can you see essence as well?" I asked Lavinia. It would make things easier and relieve some of my trepidation if she could. If I'd picked up a magical boost from breaking Martin's curse like Joyce and Edith suggested, I worried that seeing residual essence might not be the only new thing I'd acquired. It had taken several months for this ability to manifest. I hated to think what else might show up in the future.

"No," Lavinia said. "But based on the information you've given me, I think I have a potion that might help." She spun around and headed toward a shelf lining the back wall behind a glass display case filled with unique jewelry and charms.

"Where would you like me to put this?" Shawna had her purse open and was pulling out the plastic bag. She gripped one corner between her index finger and thumb, holding it as far away from her body as possible.

The flyer she'd picked up from Luna's table when we'd finished chatting with her slipped out and dropped to the floor. I bent over to retrieve the pamphlet, then followed Shawna to the counter.

"You can set it right here." Lavinia tapped the glass, then reached inside a drawer and pulled out a pair of tweezers.

"We're pretty sure Priscilla was poisoned. Will this potion be able to tell us what was used?" Shawna asked.

"There are some plants that have natural magical properties," Lavinia said. "With any luck, we'll be able to determine the source of the toxin unless an enchantment was used to distort its make-up." She opened the bag and used the tweezers to pull out the packet, leaving the discarded glove behind. After placing it on top of the flattened bag, she set the tweezers aside and twisted the top off the potion bottle. "Rylee, can you still see the speckles?"

Everyone had gathered next to the counter. Bryce eased to the left, making room for me to get closer. "They're not as bright as they were earlier, but there's still a few right here." I motioned to a spot on the wrapper, being careful not to touch anything.

The lid Lavinia held in her hand was also an eyedropper. She squeezed a couple drops where I'd specified and the spots immediately turned a bluish-purple similar to the color of Priscilla's face after her death.

"Whoa, is it supposed to do that?" Bryce asked.

Surprised by his reaction, I asked, "You can see what's happening?"

"Sure can."

I received similar agreements from the rest of the group.

"Yes, but I was hoping to see green or possibly a dark orange," Lavinia said, screwing the lid back on the bottle and setting it aside.

"We were as well," Joyce said.

"This does make things more difficult." Edith's concerned tone wasn't reassuring, nor did it help alleviate my stress.

"Why is that?" Jade glanced between the sisters and Lavinia.

"Because if it had been one of those colors, we could have narrowed it down to a couple of plants whose leaves are poisonous when brewed. Very few people in our community possess that kind of knowledge or the experience to use them."

Fewer people would have lowered the number of suspects considerably. "So what does this blue color mean, then?"

"It means an everyday sleeping potion was used," Edith said.

I'd forgotten that she and Joyce were also experts at potions until she'd spoken. "Potions are liquid, right? Wouldn't that have made the coffee grounds lumpy?"

"Some potions are derived from plants," Lavinia said. "Dried leaves can be ground into a powder."

"And a powder could easily be disguised in the coffee," I said.

"That's correct," Lavinia said. "It wouldn't be difficult to slip some of the crystals inside the packet underneath the seam where they wouldn't be noticed."

I assumed by the way Joyce and Edith were sharing a smirk they remembered the proposed theory about death by coffee that they'd shared with us earlier.

"Okay, say you're right, and our killer used leaves to make a sleeping powder, then why did they kill Priscilla instead of knocking her out?" Jade asked.

Lavinia swept her hand over the coffee packet. "The brilliance of the color signifies the strength of the amount of powder used to dose the coffee."

"That's pretty bright," Shawna said. "They must have used a lot of powder."

"I agree." Lavinia frowned at the wrapper. "Whoever did this was either inexperienced and miscalculated the amount, or they knew exactly what would happen with a dose this strong."

"In other words, we're still no closer to figuring out the person or persons responsible." I guess I'd been hoping for a miraculous revelation and was frustrated when I didn't get one.

"So we made the trip here for nothing," Myra whined. She might be extremely perceptive, but she wasn't known for being tactful when sharing her observations.

"No, that's not entirely true," Bryce said. "We've confirmed that Priscilla was poisoned and what was used." Being supportive was one of the things he had in common with his sister, so I flashed him an appreciative smile.

Bryce placed the book he'd selected on the counter, then pulled a wallet out of his back jean pocket. "Lavinia, how much do I owe you?"

While money exchanged hands, I circled the group to

hand Shawna her flyer. I was about to suggest that it might be time to go when two of the ten pictures printed on the back caught my attention. With my limited expertise in dog breeds, I knew one of the photos was a terrier, and the other was a Pomeranian. Though the dog looked a lot like Poppy, the name printed underneath confirmed it wasn't her. The images were familiar and it took me a few seconds to remember I'd seen them on the missing pet posters in the expo registration area.

There were times, like now, when my thoughts bounced around like one of those tiny silver balls in a pinball machine. The next memory that popped into my head was the chat about the herbal remedy the woman who owned Rexie had with Melanie. "Lavinia, can the powder used to make the sleeping potion be made into an herbal supplement and given to animals, say for instance, to calm a dog?" I was reasonably sure I already knew the answer but wanted clarification anyway.

"Yes, but I wouldn't recommend using anything that wasn't specifically designed for pets by professionals that know what they're doing," Lavinia said.

My mind jumped to what Wes had said about stolen show dogs when he'd first arrived to question us about Priscilla, and had my pulse quickening. If Dylan had something to do with Priscilla's death, the phone call made it sound like he had a partner. I now knew Luna had a connection to the missing animals because their owners were her clients. I was holding the proof in my hand.

Melanie's mention of an herbal supplement for animals didn't mean she was connected, but I couldn't ignore her as a possible suspect. Now I needed to find out if I was right and one or both of the women were involved.

"Guys, I think it's time to leave." I headed for the door, then paused after realizing I'd forgotten something. "Lavinia, thank you so much for your help."

"It was my pleasure. Feel free to stop by anytime." She flicked her wrist. "Now go." It was almost as if she could read my mind and knew why I wanted to leave.

"Rylee, what's going on?" Jade asked as she rushed after me with the rest of the group trailing behind her.

"We need to get back to the hotel," I glanced over my shoulder as I turned the door handle. "And hopefully prevent another crime."

"Are you saying someone else is in danger?" Bryce must have thought Priscilla had arrived and shared some ghostly incites with me. He was glancing around the same way Shawna did when she thought one of my visitors had appeared.

"Not that I'm aware of. I think I might have figured out what the killer was after, and if I'm right, they haven't finished what they started."

CHAPTER SIXTEEN

The drive back to the hotel didn't take long. Either my theories about Priscilla's killer, which I shared with the group, kept me busy, or Edith broke several speeding laws without getting caught.

The one thing we all agreed upon was that Priscilla's death had to be connected to the missing dogs, and Poppy was possibly the intended target. Of course, it was all speculation until we could prove it. Talking to Priscilla was the best place to start, but I hadn't seen her for most of the day. I was getting a little concerned since I'd expected her to pop in hours ago.

The parking spots near the front of the hotel were full, forcing us to park in a space behind the building. As I crossed the lot to reach the front entrance, I noticed a white mobile truck sitting sideways and taking up several spots. "Poochy Primper", along with a website address, was scrolled along the side in bright pink lettering, drop-shadowed in black. Paw prints, also done in black, decorated the hood and doors. There were even silhouettes of dogs and cats adorning the space between the wheel hubs.

Jade stopped next to me and asked, "Hey, isn't that the

name of Luna's business?"

Shawna took a few steps closer and drew everyone's attention to the bottom of the back door where the words "Call for In-home Appointments" was printed in black script with the same telephone number listed beneath the business name on the truck's side panel.

"A mobile business seems like the perfect way to get the layout of someone's home if you were planning to steal a pet, don't you think?" Shawna asked.

Nate wasn't wearing any gloves and stuck his hands in his coat pockets to protect them against the cold. "How much do you want to bet that if we checked on the other missing pets, we'd discover they were also Luna's clients?"

Being reminded about the stolen animals had me worrying about Barley and picking up my pace. My rational side knew I didn't need to be concerned because my cat didn't have a pedigree. The side of me that loved the little furball and couldn't bear the thought of something happening to him needed to confirm that he was all right.

As soon as we'd gathered in the lobby and I'd glanced at the check-in counter to make sure Dylan wasn't working, I lowered my voice and said, "If you all don't mind, I'd like to go check on Barley before we head over to the expo." Even if someone had said it was a problem, I would have gone anyway.

"Considering what you've discovered, I think Joyce and I would like to check on Hades as well," Edith said. "Call us if you need us. Otherwise, we'll see you all in the morning at the competition." She hurried after her sister, who was already halfway across the lobby.

I knew Jade and Shawna would go along with me without having to be asked.

"What about us?" Bryce asked, referring to Myra, Nate, and himself.

I assumed he was looking for an invite up to our room. I needed a break from the crowd to formulate a plan on how to catch Priscilla's killers. "Why don't you three head over to the expo and keep an eye on things," I said.

"We can do that." Bryce sounded as if I'd asked him to go on an undercover assignment. "Is there anything specific we should be looking for?"

"Not right now." I didn't think they knew what Amelia looked like, so asking them to find her and Poppy would be a moot request. I dismissed the idea of asking the spoofers to hang out in the animal room and monitor what Luna was doing. I worried that one or all of them would get overzealous and start asking her questions, which might ruin any plans Jade, Shawna, and I came up with to trap Priscilla's killer. As an additional precaution, I added, "We need to remain incognito. Please don't do anything suspicious."

"Remain covert. Got it." Bryce grinned, gave me a mock salute, then headed out the door with Nate and Myra.

"Good grief." Jade rolled her eyes at her brother. "Sometimes, it's hard to believe we're related."

I laughed. "Come on. We've got another mission to plan." I didn't need to see Shawna's face to know she was grinning at my choice of words. Every time we set out to help a spirit she'd acted as if we were going on a clandestine operation. I had to admit there'd been a couple times when it seemed that way.

The tag to keep the hotel staff from entering our room was still hanging on the door handle where I'd left it. Barley was curled up on the bed but jumped on the floor as soon as we entered the room. I picked him up and cuddled him against my neck. Instead of the purr I'd been hoping for, he meowed to let me know that he was way overdue for being fed. After discarding my coat and purse, I replaced his water and put food in his bowl.

While Barley happily crunched on fish-shaped morsels, my friends made themselves comfortable. Shawna sat on the end of a bed, and Jade scooted a chair away from the table and took a seat. I was too tense to sit, so I leaned against the dresser.

A few seconds later, a melodic tune echoed through the room. Since I didn't recognize the melody, I knew it wasn't my phone.

"It's mine." Shawna stretched to grab her purse where she'd placed it on the bed behind her. After sifting through the contents to find her phone, she swiped the screen. "It's a text from Nate. He says the expo is closing and they have nothing to report. They want to know if there is anything else we'd like them to do." Shawna lifted her head.

"Tell them to call it a night, and we'll regroup first thing in the morning," I said.

"Don't you want them to come up here so we can do some more brainstorming?" Shawna asked, her thumbs paused over the phone's miniature keyboard.

I didn't want to hurt anyone's feelings, but I needed a break from all the helpful yet stressful input I'd received from too many people. "I'm exhausted. Would it be all right if the three of us worked out a plan, then told the others?"

I got a "Sure" from Jade and a "Yeah" from Shawna before she sent Nate a response to his text.

"Make that the four of us," Priscilla said, appearing on the bed closest to the window. Her back was braced against the headboard, her legs outstretched in front of her. She was still a shimmering blue and was wearing the same outfit we'd found her in. The only difference was the slippers on her feet. They were brown and furry. The dog's head covering her toes had a big black nose and floppy ears.

I struggled to hold back a giggle. "Hey, Priscilla. Where have you been?" I tried not to sound like an overly concerned parent. She was already dead, and other than being trapped in this realm, there wasn't anything more that could happen to her.

"Oh, good. She's here," Jade said.

"Well, if you must know, I've been following Dylan

around all day," Priscilla stated proudly.

Curious, I pulled out the chair opposite Jade and perched on the end of the seat. "Why were you following Dylan?" I reiterated what she'd said for the benefit of my friends.

"He seemed very nervous when he let Amelia into my room to get Poppy's toys."

"Are you saying you came back while we were hiding in the closet?" I asked.

"I did."

"What was Dylan doing?" Shawna propped her elbows on her knees.

I was glad she'd asked because I wanted to know the same thing after his mysterious call.

"I'm pretty sure he was looking for the coffee packets of my special blend." Priscilla crossed her legs at the ankle. "After checking the trashcan and the counter, he made a call."

I shared the information with Jade and Shawna.

"That confirms our theory about his involvement," Jade said.

Now, all we needed to know was the identity of his partner. Priscilla knew Luna and Melanie, possibly considered them friends, and would know more about them than we did. She might even have some helpful insight that she wasn't aware she possessed.

Before I asked Priscilla what she'd learned from following Dylan, I spent the next five minutes filling her in on what I'd pieced together after viewing Luna's flyer. I also told her about our trip to see Lavinia and what we'd learned about the poison used to take her life.

"Do you think they were after Poppy?" Priscilla asked.

"Taking Poppy seems like the most logical explanation," I said.

Priscilla slumped her shoulders. "If my prized show dog was the intended target, then why am I dead?"

"It's possible whoever put the powder in the coffee

grounds only wanted to knock you out. Lavinia said the person could have been inexperienced and made a mistake with the dosage." Having to tell Priscilla her death might have been an accident made me feel worse.

"Do you still have the coffee packet?" Priscilla asked, sounding optimistic. "Can't we have the police test it for the poison to prove what happened?"

"The police already have the mug containing the leftover coffee and the wrapper from the trash can," I said to make sure Shawna and Jade continued to get the gist of my conversation with Priscilla. "They can run all kinds of tests, but according to Lavinia, the powder came from a plant with magical properties, and they won't be able to figure it out. Not unless they use a special potion like she did."

I could be wrong, but I didn't think there was a forensic team in the world that resorted to using anything paranormal to solve their cases.

Jade tapped her fingers on the table. "That's why we're trying to come up with another way to prove who was responsible."

"Catching them in the act might be our only option." Shawna hopped off the bed to retrieve her laptop. "It would be helpful if you could tell us what you learned when you followed Dylan."

"Anyone he talked to on the phone, an unusual text, or a conversation you overheard would be helpful," I added.

Priscilla got to her feet and started pacing. "First of all, I don't think Luna's involved."

"She doesn't think it's Luna," I said to my friends, then asked Priscilla, "Why not?"

"I've known her for a long time. She takes good care of the animals she grooms, even Poppy." Priscilla released a disappointed sigh. "Dylan worked at the registration desk most of the day, and during that time, he didn't talk to his sister." She stopped when she reached the foot of the bed. "He did, however, meet with Melanie behind the hotel near the dumpster during his lunch break."

"Now, that's interesting." I perched on the edge of my seat. "Please tell me you overheard the conversation between Dylan and Melanie."

"Oooh, this ought to be good," Shawna said, sitting a little straighter and taking her eyes off the computer screen. I had no idea what she was researching but assumed she'd get around to telling us if she found something relevant or important.

Presumably, Barley had finished eating because I could hear scratching in the bathroom and knew he was taking care of personal business. A few minutes later, he made his way across the room and jumped up on my lap.

"Their meeting didn't last long," Priscilla said. "Melanie asked him if he'd talked to Amelia about Poppy being at the expo tomorrow."

When I'd overheard Dylan's discussion with Amelia, I hadn't given that part of their conversation much thought. I'd assumed he was trying to be nice.

Priscilla stared at the floor. When she raised her head again, she said, "Melanie also told him they were going ahead with their plan."

I repeated what Priscilla said.

"Did either of them say what the plan was or mention any details?" Jade asked. "Are they planning to steal show dogs?"

"Nothing specific," Priscilla said. "Dylan was concerned that Wes might show up to do some more investigating. Melanie told him not to worry because she had a distraction already lined up if they needed it." Priscilla frowned. "Before Melanie left, she told Dylan to remember what would happen if he tried to back out of their deal."

I relayed Priscilla's comment, then took a moment to ponder everything she'd said.

"Melanie and Dylan must be working for some scary people if she's threatening him," Shawna said. "I wonder if they're connected to the black market."

That was a possibility I hadn't considered. A possibility that made things seem a lot more dangerous. I almost wished I could cast spells instead of only being able to see magical essence.

"You do know we'll have to involve the police eventually," Jade said. "If Logan were here, we could tell him what we've discovered and let him handle it. Since he's not, we might want to consider calling Wes."

"Everything we have so far is speculation," I said, glancing down at Barley who'd curled into a ball and gone to sleep. "He'll want to know how we found out about the conversation between Melanie and Dylan." I stroked Barley's fur, gaining comfort from his purr. "What do you think he'll say when he finds out we got the information from a ghost?"

CHAPTER SEVENTEEN

There were times when being right was enjoyable, but trying to convince Wes that I could see and speak to Priscilla hadn't been one of them. We didn't want to risk Melanie and Dylan seeing us talk to Wes and had asked him to join the spoofers, Jade, Shawna, and me first thing in the morning at a café a block away from the expo.

Out of courtesy, and because the Haverston sisters had helped by taking us to see Lavinia, I'd called and invited them along. Because of prior commitments with friends, they hadn't been able to make it and agreed to meet us at check-in for the competition instead. I'd gotten the impression from Edith that they were finished helping us, that the role they were supposed to play in our latest adventure was done.

It was a good thing Priscilla kept her promise to show up and help us with Wes. Sharing interesting tidbits about Wes's childhood that only the two of them knew was what won him over. Watching his face turn bright red and seeing him shift uncomfortably in his seat after I'd relayed an incident where Priscilla caught him in a tree spying on one of the neighborhood girls when he was thirteen was an added bonus.

After that, Wes was more than happy to hear our theories about Melanie and Dylan being the ones behind the missing pets. He'd been investigating the case without the sheriff knowing about it and had some suspicions of his own.

By the time we'd finished breakfast, we had a plan. A plan Wes decided, with Priscilla's strong agreement, not to share with the sheriff in case we were wrong and nothing happened at the expo.

We didn't know what kind of distraction Melanie had in place and hoped we could prevent her from using it. We also decided to split into teams. One to cover the inside of the expo building, the other to cover the outside.

Afraid that his presence might make Melanie and Dylan uneasy, Wes agreed to stake out the hotel parking lot in Bryce's car with Shawna, Nate, and Bryce. From there, they could watch anyone coming or going from the only entrance to the expo lot. It seemed like a logical choice since Dylan and Melanie had to eventually remove the animals from the building.

Priscilla didn't want to leave Poppy unprotected and volunteered to monitor the animal room. Jade and Myra accompanied Barley and me to the costume competition.

Most of the vendor booths were still open for shopping, but the animal room had been cordoned off and wasn't allowing any visitors. Priscilla told us they closed it because some of the owners volunteered to help out with the contest.

For a small town, Waxford had a lot of people interested in showing off their pets. When we arrived to check in, we found two separate tables. One was for cats, the other for dogs, and both with equally long lines.

Amelia and Priscilla had put a lot of thought into keeping the participants and their animals safe. The tables were placed a good distance apart, and there were several signs posted reminding everyone to keep their animals on a leash or in their carriers.

A woman I'd never seen before was helping Melanie at the table designated for dogs. Cameron and Luna were working the table for cats. Amelia was standing off to the side answering questions and directing anyone that didn't know where they were supposed to go to the appropriate line. Dylan was the only person I hadn't seen yet this morning. He wasn't working at the hotel when my friends and I left for breakfast, and I hadn't spotted him anywhere inside the expo building.

Joyce and Edith arrived before we did, and we ended up in line behind them. "Is that Hades?" I asked after noticing a leash running from Edith's wrist to the largest black cat I'd ever seen sitting on the floor near her feet.

"He's huge. What kind of cat is he?" Jade eyed him warily, no longer eager to pet him.

"He's a mixture of several breeds, the predominant one being Maine coon," Edith said.

The sisters hadn't been wrong when they'd insisted Hades was docile outside of his carrier. Even with all the activity going on around us, the cat appeared calm. Barley, not so much. I'd carried him inside, and he was squirming to get down. I was a little leery to set him on the ground next to Hades. It was either that or end up with scratches on my arms. My worries quickly faded when the only interest Hades and Barley showed in each other was taking turns sniffing backsides.

Checking in took less time than I'd expected. Once everyone was finished, Amelia picked up a wireless microphone and began speaking. "Welcome, everyone. The show will begin in half an hour, giving you time to dress your pets in their costumes. The waiting areas are behind you." She motioned toward two open doorways on the opposite side of the room. "The room on the left is for dogs, and the one on the right is for cats. Please note that once your pet is dressed in their costume, they must remain in their designated waiting area. You aren't allowed to parade them around for anyone to see, specifically not in front of the judge."

During Amelia's speech, Melanie, Cameron, and Luna had remained near the tables, no doubt to assist anyone who showed up late. Melanie seemed a little anxious. I'd glimpsed her checking her wristwatch several times after Amelia started talking.

Stressed and worried that something would go wrong, that I'd fail to fulfill my promise to Priscilla, I'd focused my attention on watching Melanie. I'd missed most of Amelia's speech but managed to catch the last part.

"Five minutes before the competition begins, someone will be along to take you to the showing arena," Amelia said. "The cats will go first, then the dogs. If your animals have trouble walking with leashes, it's okay to carry them." She smiled at the children standing closest to her and spoke with a softened voice. "Don't forget, this is all about having fun."

Some of the tension filling the room lightened, and Amelia received wide grins and eager head bobs from most of the children and their parents or family members.

Jade had the plastic bag containing Barley's costume draped over her wrist. She'd promised Shawna she wouldn't let me see his outfit until it was time to dress him and agreed to send pictures via text right afterward.

The groups of people, along with their pets, headed in the direction of the waiting rooms.

"Good luck," Edith said before following Joyce. From the serious look she'd given me, I knew she wasn't referring to the contest.

I was afraid I'd lose sight of Melanie, so I picked up Barley, and with a tip of my head, signaled Myra and Jade to step aside to let everyone else go ahead of us. When we were the last ones to reach the doorway, I glanced over my shoulder and saw Melanie heading for the vendor area.

"Now what do we do?" Jade had also noticed her departure.

I needed to follow Melanie, but putting my cat at risk

wasn't something I was willing to do. "I'll go after Melanie. You take care of Barley," I said as I placed him in Jade's arms.

Jade scowled and moved to block my way. "I'm not letting you go after her by yourself."

"Guys," Myra said, stepping between us. She hadn't spoken much since we'd arrived, and I'd almost forgotten she was there. "I'll take him." She snatched Barley away from Jade, then held out her hand and wiggled her fingers. "The bag too."

I was shocked by Myra's gesture. Taking care of my cat was one thing, but she obviously planned to show him in the contest if I didn't make it back in time. "Are you sure?"

"Cats love me." Myra snuggled Barley against her neck to prove she was right. Before I could thank her for being thoughtful, her grin transformed into a sneer. "Now go before you lose Melanie and mess up the entire operation."

"Don't bother." I stopped Jade from responding to Myra's snide comment by slipping my arm through hers and urging her out of the room.

The crowds hovering near the booths had diminished since our arrival. Even so, it looked as if we'd lost Melanie. "Do you see her anywhere?"

Jade stood in place and made a full circle. "No, not yet."

I didn't think my anxiety could get any worse. I discovered I was wrong when Priscilla appeared next to me and shouted, "Rylee!" I jumped and squeaked at the same time, causing Jade to place a concerned hand on my arm.

"Priscilla, what's wrong?" I asked with a shaky voice.

"Dylan took Poppy and Naomi's toy poodle." Priscilla waved her hands frantically. "You have to stop him."

"Where is he?" I scanned the area around us but didn't see any sign of Dylan or Melanie.

"He's taking them outside through a door at the back

of the building. Follow me," she ordered, then headed toward the room housing the animals.

"What's happening?" Jade asked. "What did Priscilla say?"

"Dylan took Poppy and Naomi's dog." I had no idea how Dylan would react when Jade and I caught up with him. Confronting him without any back-up wasn't a wise decision.

I pulled my phone out of my pocket, stopping long enough to send a text to Shawna and let her know what was happening. I'd been typing faster than normal, didn't have time to check my message, and hoped she'd be able to decipher any errors I made before hitting send.

"What about Melanie?" Jade asked. "Do you think she's working on her distraction?"

I hoped not, because as far as I was concerned, anyone that didn't have a problem stealing someone's beloved pet was capable of pretty much anything. When people were desperate and afraid of getting caught, they did dangerous things. There were a lot of bystanders in the building that could get hurt. "I don't know. Priscilla only mentioned Dylan."

Jade and I stepped over the rope strung across the entryway and attached to the portable posts sitting near each side of the door frame. Other than carriers, pet pens, and crates filled with dogs and cats, the place was empty. The lights inside the room had been dimmed, making it easier to see Priscilla's shimmering form standing in the middle of the room.

"It's back this way," Priscilla said, passing through the tables Jade and I were forced to rush around.

When Jade and I reached the exit door, Priscilla disappeared. My phone rang, alerting me to an incoming text. The message was from Shawna and said, "Be there soon."

"Looks like help is on the way," I said after showing the screen to Jade. I slipped the phone into my pocket and placed my hand on the metal bar used to open the door. "Ready?"

Jade sucked in a deep breath. "No matter what happens, we can't let Dylan leave with those animals."

"I agree." I gave the bar a determined shove.

Bursting outside was like stepping into an action-packed crime movie. Dylan must have planned to use the Poochy Primper mobile truck to transport the stolen dogs because he'd relocated it from the hotel parking lot sometime during the night. The back door was open, and Melanie was standing inside.

It seemed her plan had included stealing more animals than I'd thought because I counted a total of four carriers. Two had been placed on the floor inside the rear of the truck; the others were sitting on the pavement. The dogs inside the small cages were upset about the current situation and were barking and whining.

As soon as Melanie saw Jade and me, she hollered at Dylan, "Get in!" She rushed to the front of the vehicle and started the engine. Dylan made some angry, incoherent noises, then hoisted himself inside, slamming the door behind him.

If Bryce hadn't skidded his car to a stop in front of the truck, they might have gotten away. How far they'd have made it before law enforcement caught up with them was hard to say.

With their only avenue of escape no longer available, Dylan and Melanie didn't waste any time exiting the vehicle.

Bryce and Nate had circled to their right. Shawna was on their left with her arms outstretched, no doubt ready to initiate a ninja tackle move. With Jade and I blocking the only way back into the building, Dylan and Melanie had nowhere else to go.

"Hold it right there," Wes ordered when Melanie started inching in our direction. "You're not going anywhere." The sirens blaring in the distance reinforced his statement.

"Is that the sheriff?" I asked Wes.

"Yeah, I called him right after Shawna received your text." Wes shifted his inquiring gaze back to Dylan and Melanie. "Do you two want to tell me where you were going with these dogs?"

"Don't say a word." Melanie followed up her threat to Dylan with a glare. He clamped his mouth shut, seemingly more afraid of her than Wes.

A few seconds later, Evan arrived. It must have been his day off because he was dressed in jeans and his hair was mussed as if he'd hurried to get here after Wes had called him. It was hard to tell from his masked expression whether he was angry at Wes for allowing my friends and me to help or proud of him for solving two cases at once.

After that, it didn't take long for the handcuffs to come out and Melanie and Dylan to end up restrained and sitting on the bumper of the truck.

"Whoa, is this awesome, or what?" Shawna asked shortly after joining Jade and me.

"Not bad, that's for sure." I had to admit I enjoyed the satisfaction I got every time we solved a murder and helped a needful spirit. Thinking about ghosts reminded me that I hadn't seen Priscilla since she'd vanished.

I knew I should get back to Barley and the competition, but now that the sheriff was asking questions, my curiosity was piqued.

"Tell me again how you figured out they were the ones stealing the dogs," Evan asked Wes.

I knew Wes would have to explain how he'd gotten the information, so Jade and Shawna had helped me develop a plausible story for him to use ahead of time. An explanation that didn't include Priscilla or my ability to see ghosts.

Besides, I was happy to let Wes take the credit for catching the town's dognappers. It would save my friends and me from receiving a lecture about the dangers of investigating murders or having to hang around Waxford longer than we'd intended.

"I was over at the hotel taking the last of those statements you asked me to get." Wes patted the pocket where he kept his notepad. "Rylee and her friends were attending the costume competition and noticed these two"—he glanced at Melanie and Dylan—"removing carriers from the animal area. That's when I called you and came to investigate."

No one in our group said a word the whole time Evan scrutinized us. If the sheriff thought it was odd that Bryce's vehicle was blocking the truck and not Wes's police car, he didn't say anything.

After rubbing his chin a while longer, Evan directed his attention back to Dylan and Melanie. "Dylan, does your sister know what you've been doing? That you've been using her mobile truck to commit crimes?"

Dylan glared at Melanie. "This is all her fault," he snarled, disdain clinging to every word. "If she hadn't poisoned Priscilla, we never would have gotten caught."

"You're the one that put the special coffee packets in her room, so I'd say you're the one who really poisoned her," Melanie smirked.

"But you told me the powder you put in her coffee was only going to knock her out, not kill her," Dylan whined. "Otherwise, I wouldn't have done it."

"You wouldn't have put the packets in her room if I'd told you what I had planned." Melanie pushed off the bumper and lunged at Dylan. If Wes hadn't grabbed her by the arm and yanked her back to her seat she might have reached him.

"You're right. I'm not a murderer like you are," Dylan snapped, then dropped his head in his hands.

"I think I've heard enough for now," Evan said, glancing at my friends and me again. "You can return to the expo. I know where to reach you if I have any more questions."

CHAPTER EIGHTEEN

The sounds of shouting, growling, and barking reached Shawna, Jade, and me long before we entered the room where the competitions were being held.

"What's going on in here?" Jade asked, stopping in the entryway.

I'd expected to see the last of the contest taking place or the beginning of the awards ceremony, not cats and dogs wearing costumes and running around the room with their owners scrambling after them. If I didn't already know that Melanie was in custody, I would've believed we were witnessing the aftereffects of her so-called distraction.

"We weren't gone that long, were we?" Jade asked.

"Apparently, long enough," I said, trying to find the source of the chaos and hoping that my cat wasn't involved.

Some of the spectators had vacated the bleachers and were trying to help. I was relieved to see Myra sitting on the top bench with Barley safely perched on her lap. Joyce and Edith sat beside her, with Hades taking up a spot between them. All three women appeared to be amused and seemed to be enjoying the activity on the floor below them.

"What do you say we take a seat?" I said, heading for the stairs running along the side of the bleachers.

"Works for me," Shawna said.

"Me too," Jade said.

I climbed to the top of the bleachers, getting a better look at Barley's costume. He was dressed like a turquoise and yellow butterfly, complete with shiny wings and antennas, each with a fuzzy ball on the end. Hades was wearing a green dragon costume covered with fake orange scales and had a pair of wings even larger than Barley's. Though I couldn't see it from where I was standing, the outfit probably had a long tail hanging off the back of the metal bench.

I sat down next to Myra while Jade and Shawna took a seat on the empty bench below us.

"I take it everything went well?" Edith leaned forward and asked, even though she was smiling as if she already knew the answer.

"It did," I said. "Melanie and Dylan are on their way to the police station with Wes and Evan." I slipped the strap of my purse off my shoulder and set it next to my feet. "Bryce and Nate will be joining us shortly. They drove Bryce's car back to the hotel parking lot."

"What do you think about Barley's costume?" Shawna asked. "Cute, right?"

"Yeah, it's cute," I said and meant it. "Thanks for buying it for him." With all the holidays and annual events Cumberpatch sponsored, I figured Shawna's need to outfit my cat would have him owning more costumes than I'd collected my entire life.

"I think it's adorable." Jade reached back to scratch Barley's chin and giggled when he took a playful swipe at her.

"How did the competition go?" I asked Myra.

"The cats already went, but we're still waiting for the dogs." Myra scratched the only visible patch of fur on my cat's head. "I don't think latching onto the judge's ankle earned Barley any points, but other than that, he placed really well."

I'd never been big on competing, yet I was still disappointed that I'd missed showing Barley off in the contest. "How do you know where he placed?"

"Because they already gave out the prizes, and he took second place." Myra reached behind her seat, pulling out a silky red ribbon along with a white envelope, and handed them to me. "I also took pictures and will text them to you later."

"I'd really appreciate it." For a person that continually demonstrated snarky and skeptical behavior, Myra continued to surprise me with glimpses of her good-hearted nature. "And thank you for showing him."

Myra shrugged. "No big deal."

I stroked the ribbon's ruffled border, proudly admiring the words "Pets-R-Special Expo and Second Place" printed in gold in the center of its round surface.

"Good job, Barley." I picked him up and placed him on my lap.

"Who took first place?" Jade asked.

"That would be Hades," Joyce said, her smile beaming.

"Congratulations," I said.

Shawna shifted sideways. "He deserves it. That costume is spectacular. You'll have to tell me where you got it."

"Does anybody know what happened to cause all the ruckus?" I asked.

"As far as I can tell, that small brown terrier over there started it," Myra said.

The dog she referred to was Rexie, and the woman I'd seen talking to Melanie the day we arrived was frantically chasing after him. The dog acted like his food had been spiked with an energy booster. It was either that or he was going through the same wild animal syndrome that Barley had been experiencing.

He zipped across the floor, yapping at anything that moved. After making three laps around the room without getting close to catching him, the woman gave up, dropped on the lowest bleacher bench, and shook her head.

Finally, a woman wearing a judge's vest, who I assumed was Madelaine, entered the room. She lifted a whistle to her mouth, then blew long and hard. I couldn't hear the noise it made, but the animals certainly did. They all stopped moving long enough to give their owners a chance to catch them.

Not long after the chaos faded, and the judge gave the participants their showing instructions, Priscilla appeared at the bottom of the stairs and motioned for me to join her. She looked the way she did the first day I'd met her, and I knew it was time for her to go.

"Myra, would you mind holding Barley for a few minutes? There's something I need to take care of."

"Sure," Myra said, taking him off my lap and getting a disgruntled meow.

"What's going on?" Jade asked. "Do you need us to come with you?"

"No." I leaned forward and lowered my voice. "I need to talk to Priscilla."

They knew what was coming next and showed their support with saddened faces. After retrieving my phone and pretending I was on a call, I headed down the stairs.

"Rylee," Priscilla said as soon as I reached the bottom step. "I wanted to personally thank you before I left. Not only did you solve my murder, but this has been the most excitement I've had in years."

I wasn't good with goodbyes, even with people I didn't really know. "I'm sorry things turned out the way they did."

"I'm just glad Amelia will keep the expo running and do a good job in the process. It's the judging I will truly miss."

"Who knows, maybe they'll have dog shows wherever

you're going," I said.

"Maybe," Priscilla smiled. "You know, you're very good at solving crimes. You should consider doing it full-time. I'm sure there are a lot of ghosts that could use your help."

"Thanks, I'll think about it." At the rate Shawna and Jade were pestering me, it wouldn't be long before I'd have to make a decision about whether or not I should become a spirit sleuther.

"Goodbye, Rylee. It was a pleasure getting to know you." Priscilla's shimmering form started to fade.

"You too," I got out before she disappeared completely.

Priscilla wasn't the most annoying ghost I'd ever helped. That title still belonged to Martin. My mini-vacation had been anything but relaxing. I didn't regret the experience or the chance to help another spirit make it to their afterlife.

I was glad the weekend was almost over, and my friends and I would be heading home soon. With my ties to the paranormal world gradually increasing, I had no doubt it wouldn't be long before I found myself in the middle of another ghostly adventure.

ABOUT THE AUTHOR

Nola Robertson is an author of paranormal and sci-fi romance, who has recently ventured into writing cozy mysteries. When she's not busy writing, she spends her time reading, gardening, and working on various DIY projects.

Raised in the Midwest, she now resides in the enchanting Southwest with her husband and three adorable cats.

Made in the USA
Coppell, TX
01 April 2021